The Book of Paradise

The
BOOK OF PARADISE

The Wonderful Adventures of
Shmuel-Aba Abervo

by

ITZIK MANGER

ILLUSTRATED BY MENDEL REIF

TRANSLATED FROM THE YIDDISH BY LEONARD WOLF

 HILL AND WANG • NEW YORK

A division of Farrar, Straus and Giroux

Foreword

It is a strange thing, to be making this sad introduction to my merriest book. But perhaps, that's the way things are: at the edge of the abyss even laughter becomes desperate.

Driven from Rumania, the country of my birth, robbed of my citizenship, and exiled from my beloved Polish-Jewish community, wandering without passport or visa— in this grotesque pose I must make my bow before the public as I present to it Shmuel-Aba Abervo and his remarkable life history.

This unrestrainedly merry book contains many of my most intimate experiences and much of my own life, with its loves and sufferings.

I dedicate this book to myself as a memento of the lonely days and nights when I wandered the streets and boulevards of Paris. My most wonderful moments in that time of unending rootlessness were those meetings at night with the shadows of French vagabonds, those irrepressible singers who, in their fatherland, were, in all likelihood, no less lonesome than myself. Something of a consolation!

The Book of Paradise was to have been the first book of

a planned trilogy. It may be that *The Book of the Earth* and *The Book of the World of Errors* will never be written.

But we do not wish to cast a shadow over the merry story of Shmuel-Aba Abervo.

Shmuel-Aba, the stage is yours.

I.M.

PUBLISHER'S NOTE

Itzik Manger was living in Paris when *The Book of Paradise* was originally published in Warsaw just before the German invasion of Poland in 1939. Except for a few review copies that reached the United States, this first Yiddish edition was never distributed because the printing plant and inventory were destroyed. In 1961 the Itzik Manger Anniversary Committee celebrated the author's sixtieth birthday with a new Yiddish edition. Recent publications include a German edition published in Switzerland, a Dutch edition, and a Hebrew edition published in Israel. The present volume is the first edition in English and it includes the drawings by Mendel Reif that appeared only in the 1939 edition. The artist perished at the hands of the Nazis in a concentration camp.

TRANSLATOR'S NOTE

The narrator's little friend, Pisherl, is the only character in the book whose name needs to be understood literally. His name, in Yiddish, means "Little Pisser."

L.W.

Contents

The Book of Paradise

I

My Last Day in Eden

THE TIME that I spent in Paradise was the most beautiful of my life. To this moment, my heart aches and I get tears in my eyes when I remember those happy days.

Often, I close my eyes and live again those splendid years, years that will never return—unless the Messiah should come.

In these dreaming moments, I even forget that my wings were shorn before I was sent down to this world. I spread my arms, and I try to fly. . . . Only when I have fallen to the ground and feel a sharp pain in my bottom, do I remember that it's all too late—that only the people in Eden have wings.

And for just this reason, I have decided to tell everything that befell me—both before my birth and after it. I shall describe it, not to deceive unbelievers but to console myself. I know that many people have already described their lives in the various languages of the world. I myself have read a hundred such life histories, and I must confess that, at every point, I sensed in them human vanity—and falsehood, that falsehood which paints itself in rosy colors

1

and paints others in the darkest black. Such life histories are nothing more than a deceiving stupidity which fools especially the authors themselves.

I, on the other hand, mean to tell everything as it was, without diminishing it by so much as a hair. I'm not out to convince anyone that I was particularly virtuous in Paradise. Good Lord, no. I did my share of harm as well as good. But in my story, where I have done harm, I will say so, and where I behaved well, I shall tell accurately just how it was.

I know that many people will ask me, "How come? How is it possible for a person to remember so precisely what happened to him before his birth?" Maybe such questioners will bring evidence that such a thing is impossible. Everyone knows that just before a person is born an angel comes and gives him a snap on the nose which makes him instantly forget all of his past—even the Torah which he was studying just before his descent into the sinful world.

Those who make this point are right. Actually, that's how it is. That *is* what happens to every person before he arrives in this world. An angel does give everyone's nose a snap, and, in fact, he does forget everything. But in my case, a miracle happened—a most remarkable miracle. And I will tell about this miracle at once, so that people will not go around whispering that I, Shmuel-Aba Abervo, am spinning a yarn or turning out lies.

On that day when I was turned over to the care of the angel who was to conduct me down to this world, I happened to be sitting under an Eden tree, enjoying the canaries that had "burst into song," as the Scripture says. By the way, I should tell you that, by comparison with the canaries of Eden, earthly canaries are simply less than nothing. In the first place, the Eden canaries are twenty times bigger, and when they sing—well, it's just not possible to describe their song in any earthly tongue. One needs to hear them with one's own ears to understand the difference.

It was twilight. The Gemora teacher, Reb Maier-Parakh, an angel with heavy, dark-gray wings, had gone to the angels' prayer house for his evening devotions, and his students had scattered. Some of them were playing tag while others sat around telling stories about thieves and robbers. I went off to my beloved Eden tree to listen to the singing of the canaries.

I must confess that my greatest weakness, at that time, was the singing of the canaries of Eden. While they were singing, I could forget all the world.

So there I am, lying under the Eden tree; the canaries are singing; large butterflies are fluttering over the grass, playing tag. When I speak of the Eden butterflies, you must not suppose that they are in any way like those summer butterflies you see on Earth. If you think that, you are making a big mistake. The butterfly of Eden is nineteen times as large as those on Earth. Each butterfly is a different color—one is blue, one green, one red, another white, still another black. In short, it is not possible to describe them, since human language lacks the words for all the colors that exist in Eden.

There I am, then, lying under the tree. Suddenly, I hear a well-known voice—like a silver bell.

"Shmuel-Aba. Shmuel-Aba."

I look about and see my friend Pisherl, a mischievous little angel with intelligent, dark eyes. As always, his mouth is smeared with plum jam. He is fluttering over me with his thin, bright wings. Then he settles at my feet.

"What is it, Pisherl? What's going on? Don't keep me in suspense."

Pisherl wipes the sweat from his wings and whispers into

my ear, "Shmuel-Aba, it's bad. I've just found out you're to be sent to Earth this very day. It's your fate to become a human being. Do you know what that means? A human being!"

My heart began to beat, "Thump. Thump. Thump."

"Pisherl. What are you saying? Who told you? How do *you* know?"

Pisherl told me how it chanced that he was flying past the Eden tavern, At the Sign of the Zaddik Noah. There, in the barroom, sat Shimon-Ber, the greatest drunkard of all the angels in Eden.

"He was drinking ninety-six proof and was cursing a blue streak," Pisherl continued. "I gathered that he was in a fury because he was being sent on an errand. He's supposed to take you down to Earth, and then he's supposed to snap your nose with his finger so you'll forget everything: Eden, Torah, everything you've learned—and me, too, your friend Pisherl."

And Pisherl burst into tears. Several drops fell on my right hand. They were large and hot.

My friend's tears moved me to the point of tears. I caressed his dear head and tried to console him. "Don't cry, Pisherl. You know the kind of thing a drunken angel in a bar will say. Well, just let's see him try to take me. I'll tear out that red beard of his. I'll scratch his face up. So help me, I'll bite his red nose right off."

But Pisherl could not be quieted. He wailed at the top of his voice. "You don't know the sort of bandit he is—that Shimon-Ber. That cruel bastard."

I knew that Pisherl was telling the truth—after all, this Shimon-Ber made all the other angels tremble. He was almost never sober. To fall into his clutches was worse than falling into Hell. And yet, he was the very one chosen to take the children down to be born on Earth and to give them that famous snap on the nose.

I quivered like a fish in water. I began to imagine how it would be. This drunkard would lead me by the hand. If I were unwilling to go, he would throw me over his shoulder. Soon, we would be at the frontiers of Eden. I could already hear the drunken angel's voice, "Let's have your nose, fellow. A snap of the finger—and off with you."

In expectation of that snap, everyone shivered; they were even more frightened of it than of being born on Earth. That drunken snap of the finger had undone more than one little angel. Whenever you see a pug-nosed child anywhere in the world, you may be sure it was Shimon-Ber who caused it by snapping his nose too hard.

"Well, Pisherl. What now? What do you think? What's to be done?" I asked my friend.

"There's nothing to be done," Pisherl answered sadly. "It's too bad, but your fate is sealed. You'd never squirm out of Shimon-Ber's hands, even if you had eighteen heads. Maybe it would be best if you—"

"What? What?" I asked, looking intently into his eyes.

"If you went along with him willingly. Don't resist. And don't cry. Shimon-Ber hates being resisted. He hates tears. If you cry, you may get such a snap from him that, God forbid, you'll arrive on Earth without any nose at all. Some face you'll have then—may Shimon-Ber be cursed that way."

From Pisherl's answer, I understood that I would not be able to escape the drunken angel. All the while that Pisherl was talking, I was holding my nose, already sympathizing with my whole heart over the misfortune which, God forbid, would befall it. Deep in my soul, I was praying to the Lord of the Universe to guard and protect it.

As I was making my silent prayer to the Lord of the

Universe to protect my nose, Pisherl was sitting pensively on the grass nearby, a finger at his temple. Evidently, he was thinking something. Suddenly his intelligent, dark eyes began to sparkle. Whenever Pisherl gets an idea, his eyes glisten.

"Shmuel-Aba. D'you know something . . . ?"

"What, Pisherl?"

He looked around to be sure that no one was listening; then he whispered in my ear, "In our cellar at home, there's a bottle of Messiah wine that my father keeps (as medicine). I'll give it to you to take along on your journey."

"What do you mean—you'll *give* me the bottle for my journey," I said querulously. "Does it belong to you? And what good is it likely to do *me?*"

Pisherl smiled. "It's easy to see that you need to be led by the hand. What's so hard to understand? You'll give the bottle of wine to Shimon-Ber. He'll be so delighted with it that you can make a deal with him so he won't snap your nose too hard."

"What are you talking about, Pisherl?" I cried in a loud voice. "Do you mean to say you'll *steal?* What about 'Thou shalt not steal . . . ?' "

Pisherl burst into laughter. "Idiot, thou son of Stupid. Don't you know that 'Thou shalt not steal' is for people, and not for angels? Come on. Show me . . . tell me. Where in the Torah is it written that the Lord of the Universe commanded the angels, 'Thou shalt not steal'? Where, unless it's in the Noplace Book?"

I could see that my friend was cleverer than I, and that he was right. Just the same, I still couldn't understand. Suppose I did give the angel Shimon-Ber the bottle of Messiah wine, and Shimon-Ber then *did* give me only a light snap on the nose—still, snap it he would, and however lightly he did it, I would have to forget all that had happened to me in Eden—and that would be a great pity.

Evidently, Pisherl understood my thoughts. From his pocket, he took out a bit of clay; he began to work it with his fingers, kneading and twisting, until at last he had shaped a nose which he handed me, saying, "While Shimon-Ber is drinking the wine, you put on this clay nose. When he snaps at you, he'll hit the clay, miss your nose, and you'll escape him completely. Be sure to remember everything; and, when you are on Earth, see to it that you tell everyone that there is a Pisherl in Eden."

He rose, smoothed out his wings, and in a clear voice said, "Come. Soon Shimon-Ber will be looking for you. It will be better if you approach him yourself. But first, let's fly to my house."

That was my last flight over Eden with my dear friend.

It was not long before we alighted at the house of Pisherl's father, calf-eyed Shlomo-Zalman, the tailor with the lumpy Adam's apple. On the wall of the house there hung a sign of an angel with patched wings—to indicate that Pisherl's father was a patch-tailor who fixed wornout wings.

Pisherl went into the house and I waited outside. Very soon, he came out again, carrying the Messiah wine under a wing. He handed me the bottle and said, "Here, take it, Shmuel-Aba. And fly at once to the tavern At the Sign of the Zaddik Noah. Better for you to go to Shimon-Ber than that he should come to you."

We kissed each other, hugged each other, kissed each other again, and hugged each other once more, and who knows how long we might have continued had not Pisherl's mother, the angel Hannah-Deborah, called from the window, "Pisherl. The tripe is getting cold. Come and eat."

We kissed each other once again, and we touched wings.

Pisherl went into the house to eat his supper, and I flew off in the direction of the tavern At the Sign of the Zaddik Noah.

It was already dark in Eden. In the houses where the angels lived with their families, the lamps were burning. Bearded angels were bent over yellowed holy books. Fat lady angels with triple chins were patching shirts; young mother angels were rocking cradles, lulling the first-born little ones with song.

> Sleep my angel, sleep, my darling
> Sleep my angel, sleep, my sweet
> In your mother's cradle, darling,
> Rest your lovely wings.
> Ai, lu, lu.

As I flew by, I looked into first one, then another of the windows. I was very envious of them—the young and the old angels. They would sleep through the night, and in the morning they would wake up still in Eden. And I? Where would I be? It was sheer luck that the wind cooled the tear on my cheek, or else the tear would have burned a hole in my face.

I landed in front of the tavern. I peeped through the window and saw a couple of coarse angels, the kind that do the rough work for the Zaddikim*—plowing their fields, taking in their harvest, and getting a fig for their pains. They were sitting at small tables, drinking spirits, smoking cheap tobacco, and continually spitting at the floor through their teeth.

At a table to one side sat the angel Shimon-Ber. His red beard was disheveled, his eyes screwed up. It looked as if he had already poured a good deal into himself. The moment I saw him, my heart pounded with fear. "So, this is the

* *Zaddikim* is the plural form of the Hebrew word *Zaddik*—a man of great piety.

angel who is to lead me out of Eden," I thought. And no matter how hard I tried, I could not persuade myself to go in.

I stood thus, for some little while, undecided, until at last I got my courage up. "It has to happen sometime," I said to myself and went in.

The moment he saw me, he tried to rise to greet me with a "welcome." But he was too drunk, and his wings got twisted in some way so that he fell backward to his seat. I ran to him and helped to smoothe his wings so that, though he might not be able to stand straight, at least he would be able to fly. And, indeed, we were both in flight toward the border that separates the other world from this one.

We took off on Thursday at ten P.M., and we arrived at the border on Friday before the blessing of the Sabbath candles.

You may be sure that our flight was by no means easy. The angel Shimon-Ber, was, as I've said, thoroughly drunk. He kept losing the way, with the result that, after three hours of flying we came upon a familiar chimney—that belonging to the tavern At the Sign of the Zaddik Noah. Shimon-Ber had been drawn to the place where he usually spent his days and nights.

We all but had ourselves a little accident. The night in Eden was dark—not a sign of a star. Shimon-Ber had left his lantern in the tavern, so we were flying blind—without an inkling of where we were.

In the darkness, Shimon-Ber collided with another angel, the angel of dreams, who was, just then, flying down to Earth. In the collision, one of the wings of the angel of dreams was hurt. Shimon-Ber cursed and the angel of dreams wept. He would be unable to fly now, and the people below would have to sleep without dreams. He

The angel Shimon-Ber

limped off on one wing to Shlomo-Zalman, the patch-tailor, to get the hurt wing fixed, and we—that is, Shimon-Ber and I, continued on our way to the border.

One other result of the collision was that Shimon-Ber became a trifle more sober. He took out his pipe and stuffed it with coarse tobacco. He lighted a match and, puffing on his pipe, flew on—with me.

Every pull on his pipe created a little glow, so that, from time to time we could see where we were in the world.

We passed the Eden mill. It stood on a hill, its vanes exposed to all the winds. In Eden, many stories are told about this mill. By day, it's a mill like any other—grinding wheat and corn; but at night, it's a place for imps and devils.

I know you don't believe me. How can there be devils in Eden? I wondered that, too, when I first heard of it. I was told about them by my friend Pisherl. I myself never saw any imps or devils, but every angel will tell you what happened to Raphael, the barber-surgeon of Eden. Once, at night, when he was going to see a patient, he passed the Eden mill and heard strange cries. Suddenly, he saw before him a long tongue that an imp had put through a peep-hole in the mill. The angel Raphael cried out, "Hear, O Israel," and fell down in a swoon. He was found at dawn, lying near the mill, and was roused with great difficulty. From that time on, he suffered from a severe impediment, stuttering.

We, that is, the angel Shimon-Ber and I, flew on. Not a word was spoken between us. What Shimon-Ber might have been thinking, I can't tell. How could I know that? But what *I* was thinking and feeling, that, as you see, I do remember. And what thoughts!

I thought of my friend Pisherl, sleeping in his little bed. He is uncovered. He has kicked the bedclothes to the ground. Even in sleep, he's mischievous; there's no one like him. He's got his finger in his mouth. Who knows? He may be dreaming of me, his friend, from whom he parted today forever.

I felt like crying. Sobs were already gathering in my throat, but when I remembered that the angel Shimon-Ber hated tears, I restrained myself and let out only the gentlest of sighs.

Toward dawn, the angel Shimon-Ber became entirely sober. The morning wind was sharp and cold and we were both seized with shivers. My teeth were chattering.

"Ai, some cold," grumbled Shimon-Ber, beginning to flap his huge, cottony wings to keep warm. With every flap of his wings, he looked back in the direction of the tavern At the Sign of the Zaddik Noah.

I was not long in understanding that this was the moment to offer him the bottle of Messiah wine my friend Pisherl had given me.

"Reb Shimon-Ber," I called, frightening myself with my daring. "Reb Shimon-Ber. A good little glass of spirits would come in handy now—to warm up with, eh? What do you think, Reb Shimon-Ber?"

At the word *spirits,* the angel slapped his gray, cottony wings together with such force that he frightened a couple of blue Eden swallows that were just getting ready to sing "O, Creator of the World."

"Oh! A little glass of spirits," he cried with such a voice that ten Eden hares swooned with fright and a couple of pregnant lionesses miscarried on the spot.

From under my right wing, I took the little bottle of Messiah wine, and showed it to him. He did several loop-the-loops in the air from sheer joy. At first, I thought he had gone out of his mind. And, for a moment, I was frightened. Dealing with a crazy angel is no small matter. To this day, I shudder when I remember the young angel Pearl, who went insane because of an unfortunate love affair. O Lord, what a fuss she kicked up. She all but turned Eden topsy-turvy.

But to conclude. As soon as Shimon-Ber saw the bottle in my hand, he flew up to me, snatched it away, pulled the cork with his teeth, and began to slurp. You ought to know, by the way, that Messiah wine is heavy. Each drop weighs two and a half pounds.

"D'you know what, Shmuel-Aba?" he said. "Let's go down for a bit. We can still manage to get to the border in time." He took out his brass watch and studied the red face of the dial. We came down on a field in Eden.

When Shimon-Ber had finished swilling all there was in the bottle he became very jolly. He pinched my cheek and said gruffly, "You're a fine fellow, Shmuel-Aba."

We resumed our journey and said our morning prayers in flight. At precisely five o'clock in the evening, we arrived at the border. At its farthest edge, Shimon-Ber ordered me to stand on one foot and to recite all the Torah that I had learned. I did as he ordered. When I had finished, he took out a huge pair of shears and began to clip off my wings. While he was clipping, I managed to stick on the clay nose. He was so drunk from the Messiah wine that he noticed nothing.

"Now, let's have your nose, and let's give it a snap."

"Reb Shimon-Ber," I said, pleading, "please. A light snap, Reb Shimon-Ber." In fact, I had found favor in his eyes and so he gave my nose so gentle a snap that I all but did not feel it.

"And now—off with you."

I looked back for the last time. I saw the entire panorama of Eden as it was being dipped in pure gold. I took a final look at my wings lying on the ground.

"Good-by, Reb Shimon-Ber," I said to the angel with the cottony wings, and I descended.

II

~~~

My Birth

MY BIRTH was difficult for my mother. She wept and she shrieked and she cursed my father with ferocious curses. "Murderer. Robber. Cutthroat." My father turned even paler and wandered about the house plucking at his small black beard, wondering why my mother regaled him with such fine nicknames.

He cast frequent prayerful looks at the midwife, Sosyeh-Deborah, a woman with swollen hands and a masculine voice. Apparently, the midwife understood what his looks signified. Under her breath, she kept up a continual grumbling. "How can I help it? You can see it's a stubborn brat and doesn't want to be born."

Sosyeh-Deborah was telling the truth. She had tried various remedies. She had tried, by fair means or foul, to persuade me to be born, but none were of any use. I paid no more heed to her than to the cat and rejected her suggestions contemptuously. I laughed at all of her promises—at the "golden watch" and the "soccer ball" she would buy me the very moment I should see the light of day.

I knew that the midwife was a great liar. Stories about

her were widespread in Eden. Even my friend Pisherl had warned me that she was not to be trusted "from here to there"—indicating, as he said this, the length of his little fingernail. The memory of my friend's warning was still clear in my mind, and I kept myself alert not to yield by so much as a hair. "Well. Let her howl like a dog," I thought, and I was pleased at her frenzied gestures and her disheveled hair.

In the end, I triumphed and she went away angry, catching up her shawl and slamming the door. I laughed till my sides ached.

My father stood in a corner, frightened to death. "What now?" he muttered, wringing his hands. I felt God's own pity for him, but I would not help him. I knew that the moment I gave in to pity, all was lost.

It was Friday night, as I've said. The men had gone to the synagogue to pray, but my father was still standing in a corner of the room, like a lost man. Then, apparently realizing that there was no point in waiting for me, he too went off to the synagogue.

My mother was left alone in the house. She had no more strength left for shrieking, and there was no one left to curse. Worn with weeping, she lay on the bed.

The sight of her moved me deeply. "After all," I thought, "a mother is a mother." Nevertheless, I was still afraid to come into the light of this world. My fear of being born was greater than my pity for her.

In the other Jewish homes, the women had already lighted the Sabbath candles, but in our house the brass candlesticks stood shamefully dark. My mother looked at the candlesticks; dusk had already fallen, and she was still lying in bed as if it were an ordinary week day, not Friday evening. All at once, she lifted herself up. No. She would not disgrace the Sabbath lights. Crawling out of bed, she went slowly to the table where the candlesticks stood. I watched every move she made, everything she did, and I must confess that I was much pleased by her piety. She lighted the candles and made several gestures over the flames. Then she covered her face with her hands and whispered something I could not hear.

I was watching my mother bless the Sabbath lights for the first time. I was so deeply moved that I made the decision, come what might, to be born. I wondered how it was to be done, and decided that I would enter the new world on tiptoe—so silently that even my mother would not hear. I wanted to surprise her pleasantly for the pain she had endured on my account.

She continued standing with her face covered by her hands, whispering . . . whispering piously. I crept out so silently that, in fact, she noticed nothing.

I stood behind her, waiting for her to stop whispering and for her to take her hands from her face before I should call myself to her attention. I waited and waited. Every moment seemed a year; but my mother had no idea what a welcome guest stood behind her.

Finally, my waiting was rewarded. She took her hands from her lovely, tearstained face. My heart leaped wildly, like a bird. I could no longer contain myself and I said, "Good Sabbath, Mother."

She could not believe her eyes. For a few moments, she stood astonished. I could see her beginning to gasp for breath. Already, I regretted the trick I had played on her.

Then, her eyes lighted up. Her face beamed. She put her arms out wanting to catch me up and embrace me, to kiss me—as is the custom of all mothers. But I would not permit it. Quickly, I withdrew into the alcove where there was a pan of water. I washed, dried myself with the towel,

Good Sabbath, Mother

and only then did I go to my mother, to whom I said, "Now you can hug and kiss me to your heart's content."

She caught me up in her arms, caressed and kissed me on the forehead. She kissed each of my little limbs, and my hair—all the while calling me a variety of pet names. "Little treasure . . . my golden one . . . my crown . . . my little angel."

What pleased me most was the way that she called me her "little angel." Pisherl's mother called him that, and all the mothers of Eden used that name for their children.

My mother wanted to put me into the cradle that stood near her bed. I suppose she thought that I was tired from my long journey. I thanked her for her consideration, which continued to please me. "Thank you, Mother dear. But I really don't want to sleep yet. I'd like to wait until Daddy comes home from the synagogue. I want to hear him making the Sabbath blessing." My mother was overwhelmed with delight at what I had said and wanted to hug and kiss me again.

"My bright little *kaddish*.* May you live a hundred and twenty years." Her word *kaddish* made me sad. It reminded me that earthly mothers die. Already, I was grieved that my mother would have to die. From the first moment I saw her, I loved her; I was instantly jealous of Pisherl whose mother would never have to die.

My mother did not know what was making me sad. She gazed into my eyes and tried to cheer me up by making clucking sounds with her lips. I looked into her blue eyes, into her lovely, beaming face . . . but the portentous feeling would not leave me.

Suddenly, she turned pale and slapped her hands together. "Oh, you foolish mother. I completely forgot." She

---

* *Kaddish*. The memorial prayer for the dead. Also, a boy or a man who says the prayer. Here, it is simply an affectionate word meaning "son."

ran to the dresser, opened a drawer and busied herself, searching about until at last she found two pieces of ribbon. She bound one of the ribbons around my right hand and the other around my left. They were talismans against the evil eye. I was delighted with the ribbons and began to play with them. I tried tearing them from my wrists without success.

My mother watched me playing. She enjoyed my grimaces and laughed heartily at them. Finally, I became bored with the ribbons and turned my head toward the Sabbath candles on the table, where I saw two moths hovering near the flames. At any moment, they would burn.

"Mother, tell them not to get too close to the flames or else, God forbid, there'll be an accident."

My words prompted my mother to catch me up in her arms once more. "What a darling child you are. May you live well and happily, dear soul." I was distressed that she was kissing me instead of warning the moths which, meanwhile, were perishing in her Sabbath candles.

My mother noticed that my mood was cloudy, and understood that I was annoyed with her. She began making excuses. "Don't be angry, my treasure. Don't be vexed with your mother."

Sternly, I told her that I was indeed angry with her—very angry that, because of her carelessness, two creatures had died. "You should have warned them, Mother. It was your duty to warn them. Why didn't you warn them?"

She stared at me, astonished at my words. "What do you mean, my child? Would they have understood me, even if I *had* said anything? I don't know their language any more than they know mine."

What my mother told me was indeed news. On Earth, God's creatures did not understand each other's language. Suddenly, I sensed what troubles could come from such confusion. I felt the limitations of all earthly creatures and I pitied them greatly.

My mother stared into my eyes. I knew she was not to blame. She had been unable to talk with the moths. It was I who was the truly guilty one; I, who was able to speak their language and had not spoken. I had wanted my mother to have the grace of the good deed for the sake of the "Honor thy father and mother" commandment. The result was that I had committed a great sin.

I consoled my mother, calmed her, and begged her to forgive my anger. "You understand, Mother," I said, "I'm a little tired and nervous from the long journey."

My mother forgave me on the spot. Like all earthly mothers, she did not need to be pleaded with. She caressed my head with her soft hand; then she asked me again, "Wouldn't you like to rest, darling? Come. Lie down in your cradle. Mommy will sing you a lullaby."

I could see the lullaby already trembling on her lips, and though I was very curious to hear it, still, I pleaded with her. "I'm all right, Mother. Please let me wait until Daddy comes home from the synagogue. I want to hear how he blesses the wine. I want to spend my first Sabbath evening at table with my parents. And after supper, I'll join my father in the Sabbath songs."

My dear mother said nothing more. She rose, and, from a cupboard, took a bottle of wine and two small glasses— one for my father and one for me. Then she seated herself at the window to wait for my father.

A star was glittering at a windowpane—a pious Friday evening star. It looked rather familiar to me. Softly, so my mother would not hear, I asked it to give my regards to Pisherl.

My mother looked out of the window. I sat in a chair watching her. I could not get over my wonder at her lovely features. All at once, she turned to me, put a finger to her lips, and said, "Shhh. Your Daddy's coming."

I ran up to her and begged her not to tell him I was there. I would hide in the closet from which I would come out without warning.

My mother agreed. On that first Friday night, she agreed to everything I wanted. No sooner did I hear my father's step, than, quick as a wink, I was inside the closet. With a hearty "Good Sabbath," my father opened the front door.

I studied my father from the closet. He was a man of middle height with a black beard, dark eyes, and a wrinkled forehead. It was a face full of woes. What displeased me about him was this: he had a nasal voice.

My father paced the floor, saying *"shalom aleichem"* to the angels that might be in his house. I looked everywhere, but I saw no signs of any angels. With a pious face, my mother stood by, listening to my father's nasal *shalom aleichem*. It made me angry. I thought he must be either a liar or a fool. How else could I interpret his moving about the room talking to angels when, if one's life were to depend on it, there were none to be seen.

My father poured himself a glass of wine and began to make the Blessing of the Wine. Quietly, I crept out of the closet. I approached the table on tiptoes, and, at the very moment when my father was bringing the wine glass to his lips, I took my glass in my hand and, in full voice, started, in my turn, to say the blessing.

My father's glass fell from his fingers. He stood bewildered, looking now at my mother, now at me, and, as it appeared, understanding nothing. "God love your guest," my mother said, pointing at me. "Why are you staring, Faivl? It's our *kaddish;* our only son."

My father continued to stand like one stunned. Slowly,

I began to sing

slowly, he came to himself. Stretching a hairy hand out, he greeted me with his *shalom aleichem.*

"*Aleichem shalom* to you, Daddy," I replied, and we seated ourselves at the table.

My mother served the meal, casting occasional glimpses at us. The sight of my father and me together at table gave her great joy. She murmured quiet wishes to herself that her happiness might not be spoiled.

All through the meal, we were silent. My father and I exchanged not so much as a word, though from time to time we looked at each other appraisingly and went on eating. I could see that my father was wondering how it was that I could manage my fork and spoon like a grown-up. He had no idea that I could still remember all the Torah I had learned in Eden. And indeed, how could he have understood such a thing, since we had not as yet exchanged two words.

I noticed that my mother ate almost nothing—a tiny swallow of soup, a small bite of meat, and the smallest crumb of bread. It was enough for her that I was eating heartily, thank God. She could not take her eyes from me for a moment as I ate right along with my father.

He began to sing the Sabbath songs, but his singing did not please me at all. I recalled the Sabbath evenings in Eden, and the songs that were sung there and my heart ached.

Evidently, my father did not know what I was thinking. He continued to sing his nasal songs as if he were performing God knows what feats. I felt such a strong disgust rising in me that I thought I would faint away at any moment. Finally, I could stand it no longer and cried out, "Daddy. Do you know what? Let me sing a little by myself."

My father turned red. A vein in his temple began to

throb. He raised his hand and offered to hit me—as a father can.

At that moment, my mother chanced to be in the kitchen, and who knows whether he might not have socked me so hard in the jaw that, as the saying goes, I'd have seen stars for a week. Luckily, I had already begun to sing. My father's hand remained suspended in the air and stayed that way until I finished my song.

As I sang, all the birds in the city gathered outside our windows, on our roof, or wherever there was a bit of space available. My mother stood on the doorsill with a cooking pot in one hand, wiping her eyes with the other.

The flames of the Sabbath candles danced, continually bending toward me. They greeted me as if I were a dignitary of the highest sort. The cat had been about to wash its kittens but now it stopped with its tongue hanging out.

Reb Shmuel-Zainvl, our neighbor, who had just been swallowing some noodle soup, was left with a noodle dangling from his beard. His soup spoon arrested in his hand, he listened, transfixed by my singing. Men, women, and children gathered outside our door and at our windows. They stood, their ears cocked, fearful lest they miss something. The men clutched their beards, the women clasped their bosoms, and the children stuck their fingers in their mouths.

The deaf shachna shouted to deaf Berl so that everyone, including him, should hear, "It has the true taste of Eden." Deaf Berl agreed. Yes, he had heard nothing like it in all his days. And he, deaf Berl, was not just anyone. He had heard a great deal in the course of his lifetime.

The Orthodox priest swore later that the apple trees in his garden bloomed on that Friday night. Not only that, but the apples turned ripe in an instant and fell to the ground.

I don't recall how long I sang. I only remember that at the precise moment when I stopped, my father's hand fell. Clearly, he had forgotten that he had raised it to slap me. From my mother there flowed an entire river of tears. Had I sung for another half hour, she would have drowned the house entirely.

No sooner had I ended my singing than all the birds scattered, each bird to its nest. The cat finished washing her kittens, and our neighbor finished eating his noodle soup.

The door opened and a crowd of people pushed into the house. I had my first glimpse, in this life, of endless beards and gabardines. "Who was it who sang so beautifully, Reb Faivl?" they asked my father. My father, pointing his finger at me, replied, "It was he, my son. That is, my son who was born this evening."

"Then you are to be congratulated, Reb Faivl," they said, and they congratulated my father and mother.

Everybody greeted me with *shalom aleichem* and expressed the wish that I would grow up to be a pious Jew. My hand hurt from all the handshakes that accompanied the *shalom aleichems,* and still the door opened. No sooner did one group leave, than another entered. Their congratulations stunned my ears and the handshakes nearly lamed my hand.

Fortunately, my mother finally interfered. She could no longer stand to see me in pain, and cried out, "You might leave the child in peace. Be kind enough to come another time. At his circumcision feast, God willing."

It was some little while, nevertheless, before the people finally left. When I was alone with my parents, I said, "After sunset tomorrow, will you be good enough to invite the rabbi, the rabbinical judge, and the richest man in our village. I want to tell them and you what I saw and heard, as well as what I experienced, in Eden."

Once more, my father was rendered speechless. At last he said, with difficulty, "What do you mean, you'll tell us about Eden? Do you remember what happened there? Didn't the angel snap your nose to make you forget?"

I assured my father that I remembered everything precisely, and that I had forgotten nothing. And in order to demonstrate that I was telling the truth, I related the story of the angel Shimon-Ber who had conducted me from Eden to the boundaries of this world.

My father was beside himself. He would not let me alone for a moment. Over and over again he inquired about, and checked, the most minute details. Again and again I told him what had happened, and, certainly, we would have gone on in this way all night had not my mother interfered.

"Faivl. Why are you tormenting the child? You can see he's tired. Tomorrow is another day. You'll have time enough to talk to him as much as you like. Come, little darling. Come to bed."

My mother gathered me in her arms, laid me in the cradle, and covered me. And as she rocked the cradle, she sang her lullaby for the first time. For a while, I lay there with open eyes. But at last, the rocking of the cradle and my mother's singing lulled me to sleep.

III

My First Sabbath on Earth

ON SABBATH MORNING, my father got up early. Having waked even earlier, I lay in my cradle watching everything he did.

I had watched the sunbeams with wonderment as they crept into the room from different directions, one from the east wall, the other from the west. They had crept slowly, approaching each other until they met and greeted each other over my father's bed. And boom! They had fallen into my father's beard.

My father woke and shook his beard. The sunbeams fell to the ground. I was entranced by the entire byplay.

My father jumped out of bed and began to dress. One, two, and he was done. He washed his hands and began to pace the room. Unless I miscounted, it was some two hundred times. Finally, his pacing bored him. As I watched, he approached my cradle. Quickly, I closed my eyes.

My father stood looking down at me, wondering, perhaps, whether I took after him or my mother. Then I felt him nudging me. "Get up," he said. "Enough snoring. Time to go to the synagogue."

I shut my eyes more tightly, pretending to be asleep. I must confess that I was enjoying my mother's cradle, and I had very little desire to go to the synagogue.

But my father was determined. He poked me harder and harder and all but shouted, "What does it take to wake you, you so-and-so."

The noise he made woke my mother. From her lovely eyes, there flashed an angry look, then she really tore into him. "What do you want of the child? Who ever heard of taking an infant, born only yesterday, to the synagogue? Do you hear me? Leave the child alone, at once. You . . . *shlimmazel.*"

At the word *shlimmazel*, my father seemed to shrink. He could never stand up to my mother's anger. Smiling a foolish smile, he said apologetically, "If not—is not. If you say 'no,' let it be 'no,' Zelda." It was from him, and at that moment, that I learned that my mother's name was Zelda.

My father thought he had now escaped her wrath, but he was much deceived. Imitating his tone, my mother said, "If not—is not. Just look at him, the *shlimmazel*. He hasn't sense enough to know that one doesn't drag an infant to the synagogue. What a *shlimmazel*. You'd have to search the whole world over to find his like."

My father stood as if he had been whipped. He was utterly unprepared for such treatment, particularly on a Sabbath morning and on an empty stomach. He snatched up his prayer shawl and went off to the synagogue, making his escape.

My mother jumped out of bed and put her clothes on. She bent over the cradle and stroked my head.

"Sleep, darling, sleep, my dear. May your bones prosper." Catching her hand, I began to kiss it. I was thanking her for having rescued me. I said, "Dear Mother, thank you. May you live for a hundred and twenty years. Thank you for putting Daddy in his place. He was jealous because I was still asleep, so he woke me."

The fact is, I was telling my mother a lie. Satan (may his name be blotted out) urged me to it. Instantly, I regretted my lie, but shame prevented me from confessing at once, as I wanted to do.

By the way, that was the only incident of that Sabbath morning. In other respects the day went along like all Sabbaths, a little festive, a little dull. My father came back from the synagogue. We ate. My father had a little nap and my mother read the woman's Bible. Let me say that, of all the Sabbath delicacies, I was most pleased by the bean-and-barley soup—the one dish on earth with the true taste of Eden.

My father was snoring; my mother was whispering over her woman's Bible. The summer flies were buzzing at the windowpanes. My eyelids grew heavy and, at last, I fell asleep, only to wake again at evening. It was already dark in the house. My mother was softly and piously saying her "God of Abraham" prayer.

My mother's prayers roused in me a persistent yearning. To return . . . to return to Eden. I recalled once more the Sabbath twilights of Eden. There, in the Three Patriarchs' Allée, the girl angels stroll, casting eyes at the passing boy angels. You ought to be told, by the way, that in Eden nobody flies on the Sabbath. Everyone goes about on foot.

My mother was sitting in her corner, whispering "God of Abraham, Isaac, and Jacob." In my mind's eye, I was seeing the patriarchs strolling through Eden. Father Abraham was walking pensively, his hands behind his back. Father Isaac was wearing a pair of dark glasses (his eyes continued to be weak) and Father Jacob was incessantly taking out his snuff box, taking a sniff and sneezing so loudly that he could be heard all over Eden.

Everyone in Eden was tremendously envious of the three patriarchs, each of whom owned a fine villa with a garden, not to mention other large parcels of land which the peasant angels worked for them.

I remember one of those Sabbath twilights in Eden. The patriarchs, as was their custom, were strolling in the Three Patriarchs' Allée. They were talking among themselves; indeed, they were getting rather heated. I was awfully curious to hear what they were talking about. "No doubt," I thought, "they are talking about the holy Torah. It will be worth listening to."

I said to my friend Pisherl, who was with me, "Do you know what, Pisherl, let's eavesdrop on the patriarchs' conversation." He agreed at once. His intelligent dark eyes glittered. "Come on, Shmuel-Aba. Let's listen." Taking each other by the hand, we stole silently after the holy patriarchs. They were so deeply engrossed in their conversation that they did not even notice us.

"Take my advice," the patriarch Isaac was saying, "and divorce the two maid servants if you want peace in the house. Can't you see that neither Rachel nor Leah can endure keeping house with your mistresses. The quarrels of your household women are the shame of Eden."

The patriarch Abraham, who was walking on the right, nodded, agreeing that Isaac was right. "It's not fitting, Jacob. Do you hear? Drive the maid servants away."

"Grandpa," countered the patriarch Jacob, "I won't do it. I lived out a lifetime with them on earth. I've succeeded at last in getting them admitted to Eden; then how can I drive them out of the house now. Where's the justice in it, Grandpa?"

"Justice, shmustice," said the patriarch Abraham with a gesture of his hand. "You do what your father and your grandfather tell you. They mean well by you."

"The Hagar story—twice over," said Jacob angrily. "I will not and I shall not do it. If they like, the women can scratch each other's eyes out."

Evidently, Jacob's reference to Hagar grieved the patriarch Abraham. He turned red as a beet and shouted, "Boor. Is that a way to talk to your grandfather?" With that, he gave Jacob a tremendous slap.

I was very frightened. Catching my friend Pisherl's arm, I said, "Come, Pisherl. Let's run. I hate fighting. Here I was hoping to hear a little Torah, and now look—they've come to blows."

Pisherl smiled. "Anything to please you, Shmuel-Aba."

"Well then, let's go to the Eden tree and listen to the canaries."

"Good, Shmuel-Aba. Let's go."

On the way to the canaries, I asked my friend, "Do you think the patriarch Jacob will really drive them away?"

"Who knows?" Pisherl said, his eyes twinkling. "The patriarchs are very stubborn. We'll see what we'll see."

My mother had lighted a candle and was just wishing us a good week, but I was so engrossed in my thoughts that I didn't hear her. She came to me and looked into my eyes. "What are you thinking, lambkin?"

"Nothing, Mother. Just musing a little." I sensed that I ought not to tell her of the unpleasant little scene in Eden. She was a pious woman, my mother, and it would only make a disturbing impression on her.

But she would not let me be. That mother of mine insisted on knowing what I was thinking. I was faced with a dreadful dilemma. Fortunately, I recalled a second story of something that had happened in Eden. I said, "I was just remembering how the patriarch Jacob pinched my cheek once in Eden."

"Tell me about it, darling."

"What is there to tell, Mother? The patriarch Jacob went one night to say his prayers in the patriarchs' synagogue. Evidently, his shawl was badly pinned to his caftan and it fell to the ground. I picked it up and handed it to the patriarch. 'Reb Jacob. You dropped your shawl. Here it is.'

"The patriarch took the shawl and asked, 'Which Bible chapter is being read this week?'

"I replied, 'And he lived . . .'

"Then he pinched my cheek and said, 'You're a good lad.' And went on his way."

"Which one—which cheek did he pinch?" my mother asked, her eyes radiant.

"This one. The left cheek—right here." I pointed.

My mother kissed the spot some thousand times. Nor were these her usual kisses. There was a pious trembling in each kiss. After all, just imagine! It's no small thing: The fingers of the patriarch Jacob himself had touched her son's cheek.

My mother was a good and pious woman. With all my heart, I wished her well of her joy.

My father came home from the synagogue, and the benediction over the wine began. I watched the ceremony with interest. When he was finished, I asked him, "Are the people I asked you to invite coming?"

"I'm expecting them at any minute," replied my father. "But be respectful of them. It's no small matter to be visited by such people as Reb Yeshaya, the rabbi; Reb Zaddok, the rabbinical judge; and Reb Mikhel Hurvitz, the local rich man. They're the best people in town."

I promised my father that I would be respectful of the best people in town and that I would behave myself.

"And in the name of God," my father added, "tell the

The patriarch Jacob pinched my cheek

truth, and nothing but the truth. Do you hear?" I felt insulted.

"What do you take me for?" I asked him. "Am I some sort of nobody who tells lies?"

My mother (blessings on her head) also joined in the battle. She was always ready to interrupt my father; particularly now, when she saw that he had insulted me. "Faivl, what do you want of the child?" she said furiously. You suspect him of telling lies, without any rhyme or reason. Have you ever caught him in a lie? Tell me. Go on. What are you staring at?"

My father wanted to reply, or to put it better, to justify himself, to say that, God forbid, he had not meant anything bad; that he had only meant . . . "You know what I meant, Zelda."

But my mother would not let him finish. Only she was to be allowed to speak. Once the storm began, she would not let up for a minute, but drove on to victory. "Just look at him, that fine father; he thinks even an infant tells lies. You're a fine father. A father? A stone. That's what you are. A plague. A dragon. But not a father."

I was in ecstasies at her calling my father a dragon. He stood confounded. It was his second portion of grief that day, and it was only the beginning of the week. He stammered, "I didn't mean anything . . . that's enough, Zelda."

Watching my father as he stood, so lost and helpless, I was very tempted to cry "Dragon" right in his face, but luckily, I remembered the commandment, "Honor thy father . . ." and I restrained myself.

My father took a Bible from the bookcase. He sat down at the table and began to turn the yellowed pages. I had the impression he was hiding his face for shame. My mother went to the kitchen to light the samovar and to get ready for the guests who were expected at any minute.

I sat on the floor, watching my father's shadow moving back and forth along the wall. It was three times larger than he was himself. I wondered curiously whether his shadow was as cowardly as he was. And what would happen if his shadow were to meet my mother's on the wall. Some wedding that would be! It would have been most interesting to see.

I crawled to my father's bench, and, out of idle curiosity, I began to tickle his foot. I tickled slowly at first, then more quickly. He was instantly ready to give me a smack or two, but at that moment, my mother came in with the boiling samovar. He sat down again as if nothing had happened.

Soon after this, the dignitaries arrived. The rabbi came first; behind him, the rabbinical judge; and finally, the rich man, Reb Mikhel Hurvitz. They congratulated my father and mother and greeted me.

I looked them over. The rabbi pleased me most. He was a small, lean Jew with a white beard. His hands trembled, but there was a twinkle in his myopic eyes. The rabbinical judge was somewhat taller than the rabbi and a good deal younger—somewhere in his forties. He had a mole on his left cheek. He spoke gently, unhurriedly, taking pleasure in every word he uttered. Reb Mikhel Hurvitz, the rich man was a thickset fellow with a close-cropped beard who did not appeal to me very much. He seemed to be a little overostentatious, with gold rings on his fingers, a gold chain, a gold watch and a mouthful of gold teeth. What distressed me was the respect with which the rabbi and the rabbinical judge treated him though he was not much of a learned man.

The guests seated themselves at the table. The rabbi sat

opposite me, watching me with his weak eyes, wondering at the way I sat, as if I had been an adult. For a while, they all kept silent. My mother stood to one side, lost in admiration of me. Anyone who has not seen my mother on that Sabbath evening has never seen loveliness.

The rabbi spoke first. Passing a hand over his long white beard, he said, "It is said that you want to tell us of Eden. Speak, then, and let us hear. What is happening in Eden?"

I stood up and replied that I was ready to tell them about all that I had experienced before my birth, but only on one condition, and that was that they, the rabbi, the rabbinical judge, the rich man, and my father must swear not to tell anyone else. I did not require my mother to take this oath because I would take her word for it that she would be silent.

Though my condition was not entirely to their liking, they had, nevertheless, little choice in the matter. Each of them had to get up, raise his hand, and say after me, word for word, "We swear by the moon and the stars that the secret forever is ours, so help us almightiest God."

After this oath, they sat down in their places, and I said to my mother, "Mother, will you be good enough to drape the windows and stuff up all the cracks in the house so that not even a breeze, God forbid, can steal in to overhear us. The breeze tells everything to everyone, without making distinctions."

My mother, a blessing on her head, immediately did my bidding. She closed all the shutters and drew all the curtains. There ensued a solemn silence. If I am not mistaken, I even saw the rabbi's beard trembling.

I put my finger to my forehead, trying to think at what point to begin. After a long moment, I decided to tell first of all how the angel Shimon-Ber had guided me out of Eden, and how I had used the clay nose. I painted Shimon-

The guests seated themselves

Ber's portrait for them, exactly as I remembered him. The rabbi held his head.

"Oh my, oh my. That an angel should be such a drunkard. How do they allow it there in Eden—eh?"

I told him how it did no good to scold Shimon-Ber. "In Eden one is used to his misbehavior; if only things move along smoothly, and he forgets sometimes to beat his wife . . ."

"He beats his wife? The monster," said the rabbi, amazed. "Good Lord. Oh, good Lord."

"And what beatings, rabbi! His wife, the angel Zissl, who is almost always pregnant, goes about with circles under her eyes and black and blue marks on her body."

"When that happens in Eden, it's the end of the world," sighed the rabbi. The rabbinical judge, the rich man, and my father sighed too.

All the while that I talked about the angel Shimon-Ber, the rich man, Reb Mikhel Hurvitz, kept continually touching his nose. It was from me that he first learned why it was that his nose was a trifle snubbed. "Hmm . . . hmm . . ." he grumbled. "Lucky for that angel that he doesn't live on earth. If he did, I'd take him to court." It should be said that the rich man, Reb Mikhel, dearly loved litigation. At the least provocation, he filed a complaint at once. In this case—himself *versus* Shimon-Ber—it would have been a one hundred per cent victory for him.

I was beginning to regret the entire situation. I thought, "What good will come of talking with this bunch of pious souls. They can't stand being told the truth." But, since I had begun, I decided to go on till the end.

Reb Zaddok, the rabbinical judge, gave a cough, and turned to me with the request that I tell him how extensive might be the boundaries of Eden. "That is to say," he added, "I am curious to know how large an area Eden occupies."

I told him that, God be praised, Eden was large enough, occupying an area of four hundred thousand square miles. On the east, it borders the Turkish Eden; on the west, the Christian Eden. On the south, it is separated from Earth by two thousand cloud curtains; and on the north, a sea of fire separates it from Hell.

"Good Lord, good Lord," cried the rabbinical judge, and held his head.

"Wonder of wonders," the rabbi said, grasping his beard.

"*Sonderbar,*" the rich man said, clutching his gold watch.

I went on, "Eden is inhabited mostly by angels and pious Jews. There are few Lithuanians, but a great number of Polish Jews. And the rest are Galician Zaddikim."

There is not much love lost between the Zaddikim and the angels. The angels argue that there are too many Zaddikim in Eden. One thousand to the square kilometer. There is hardly enough air to breathe, the angels complain, and they curse the Zaddikim darkly.

Among the Zaddikim there is hardly what one would call peace. The Polish Zaddik considers the Galician unclean, and vice versa; but they are both agreed that the Lithuanian Zaddik ought under no circumstances to be allowed into Eden.

What troubles the angels most is that the Zaddikim go around all day doing nothing, never putting so much as a hand in cold water, and ordering the angels about as if they, the angels, had been their servants from the first moment of the Creation.

Once, at a general gathering of the angels, the angel Jonah-Toib went so far as to offer a resolution to request the Almighty to abridge the rights of the Zaddikim, and to establish an entry quota for them in Eden.

Almost all the angels applauded this resolution and it would certainly have passed by a majority if the Zaddikim had not had a piece of luck. At the last moment, a yellow-haired angel named Raziel, who was something of a mystic, took their part.

He stood up and began to make a speech. What he said nobody could be sure of. He was generally difficult to understand, but one thing was sensed—that he was defending the Zaddikim and that he was against the resolution proposed by Jonah-Toib. At one point, indeed, he called Jonah-Toib an impious Jew and a Haman.

There was a wild tumult. The angel Raziel was widely respected in Eden, though many believed it was because he could not be understood, and one could never be sure how much wisdom might be lurking in his words. Everyone took sides; one side was for the angel Jonah-Toib's resolution, the other for the angel Raziel. At one moment, the two sides were very close to blows.

The final result was that the Zaddikim carried on as before in Eden, lording it about as if they were in their father's vineyard. If they were even slightly provoked, they were quick to quote the famous passage from the Song of Songs, "Kiss my . . ."

After that meeting, the angels organized themselves into two societies, I went on. One society called itself the COZ, that is, *contra the Zaddikim*. The other society called itself the PROZ, that is, *pro the Zaddikim*.

For my listeners, I sketched clearly the methods of the two groups. I told them of a whole series of pamphlets that one group wrote about the other; of the attacks that both groups made.

"Oh my, oh my," the rabbinical judge said, clutching his head.

"Wonder of wonders," the rabbi said, clutching his beard.

"Sonderbar," said the rich man, Reb Mikhel, clutching his gold chain.

Reb Mikhel, the rich man, it ought to be said, traveled frequently to Leipzig on business, and, therefore, enjoyed dropping an occasional German word into his speech.

"At least, let's hope that none of the Zaddikim were hurt," my father said, breathing gently as he watched the rabbi. I understood that look. It said, "You won't need to be afraid of getting to Paradise, Rabbi. If I were as holy as you, you'd see what I'd accomplish in Eden." My father longed with all his heart for Eden, and I could well understand why. Here on Earth, he was my mother's footstool, but there, she would be his footstool. And once he set his foot on her, he would avenge himself for all the slights she had given him on Earth.

The rabbi asked me if I had seen the Tree of Knowledge, and when I replied that I had, he sighed. The rich man wanted to know if gold coins existed in Eden. And the rabbinical judge asked me if the female angels went to the ritual baths at the appointed times.

The entire interruption to which I was being subjected began to irritate me. No sooner had I answered one question than I was beset by another.

I, myself, had caused these people to be invited so that I might tell them of my experiences in Eden; and now, all of a sudden, what did I have on my hands—an interruption! It was enough to disgust me. I lost all impulse to go on. Several times, I yawned openly; that is to say, I gave broad hints that I was tired and that I did not care to be bothered any more. But they took no notice and kept up their questions. For instance, the rabbi wanted to know if I had seen the Messiah-Ox and whether it was really so huge that it would suffice to feed all Israel at the coming of the Messiah.

I could contain myself no longer and said that I was tired and did not care to go on. I said that if they wished to come on the following evening, and if they would sit still and listen, I would tell them how I became acquainted with my friend Pisherl.

"Oh dear, oh dear. An angel called Pisherl. Oh my!" said the rabbinical judge, putting his hand to his head.

"Wonder of wonders—an angel named Pisherl," the rabbi said, clasping his beard.

"*Sonderbar,*" Reb Mikhel, the rich man, said, clasping his golden chain.

But I wanted no more to do with them. I called my mother over and told her it was high time for me to be nursed. I had had nothing to eat since four o'clock.

After my mother had nursed me and carried me to the cradle that stood near her bed, she began to rock me.

I lay still, thinking that the creatures on earth were strange indeed; and so musing, I fell asleep.

The rabbi, the rabbinical judge, and the rich man continued to sit awhile, drinking tea and talking with my father; then they left. At the threshold, the rabbi said to my father, "Well, then, God willing . . . tomorrow, Faivl."

IV

My Friend Pisherl

ON THE SECOND EVENING, when my parents, the rabbi, the rabbinical judge, and the rich man were already seated around the table, I rolled up my sleeves and resumed my narrative.

I met my friend Pisherl in the Hebrew school run by Maier-Parakh, the Gemora teacher, where we were both pupils. I liked him from the start. That little angel with the dark, intelligent eyes pleased everyone who ever met him, with the understandable exception of the Gemora teacher, Reb Maier-Parakh, whom he tormented severely.

To be truthful, the Gemora teacher had reason for being angry with my friend Pisherl. My friend all but crippled him once with a prank he played on him. It was a Tuesday afternoon and the Gemora teacher was hearing us repeat our lessons. He threatened us with his cat-o'-nine-tails, waving it over our heads, back and forth, until at last he began to snort, and finally, as was his custom, he fell asleep. The cat-o'-nine-tails fell from his hand.

Pisherl's eyes glittered. Turning to us, his fellow pupils, he asked, "Fellows, can you keep a secret?"

We replied that we could, and waited with great interest to see what would happen. We understood that Pisherl was up to something.

Pisherl took a piece of tar from his pocket. On tiptoes, he went up to the Gemora teacher, whose wings drooped wearily. Slowly, Pisherl lifted the teacher's right wing, smeared it with the tar, and pasted it down to the bench. Having finished with the right wing, he smeared the left.

We were choking with laughter, imagining the moment when the Gemora teacher would wake up. We waited and waited, but he slept on. He seemed to have no intention of waking.

Seeing that he would not wake up, my friend Pisherl went up to him and shouted into his ear, "Rabbi, time for evening prayers."

The Gemora teacher woke up and started to fly to the synagogue, wrenching the wings pasted to the bench so hard that he pulled the wing-tips quite off. He fell to the ground, yowling with pain. His wife Golda, an angel with a cataract in her right eye, flew in from the kitchen. She set up a cry, and sent at once for Raphael, the barber-surgeon angel. He, in turn, sent to the Eden pharmacy for an adhesive bandage with which he pasted the Gemora teacher's wing-tips back on.

From that time on, the Gemora teacher had it in for my friend Pisherl. He (that is, my friend Pisherl) was beaten whether he was guilty or not. But my friend was one of those pranksters whom no amount of beating could deter from playing tricks. And it was just for this reason that he was dear to me. I was bound to him, body and soul, as, in turn, he was to me. Whenever anything occurred to me, he was the first to know; and he, for his part, always consulted me.

I had but to ask, "Pisherl, what do you think . . . ?" and

Pisherl immediately put his finger to his head, thought for a while, and then came up with the right suggestion: "Shmuel-Aba, suppose you try . . ." I told him everything I thought. I hid nothing from my comrade who was as dear to me as a brother, and perhaps even dearer.

I know that you will say that the trick Pisherl played on the Gemora teacher was not particularly original. Every schoolboy on earth can brag of similar tricks played on teachers. To this, I reply, first, that this was not the only stunt Pisherl pulled in Eden and, second, that earthly schoolboys are liars, boasting of imaginary accomplishments, while Pisherl actually performed *his* tricks.

One day, Pisherl came to me. He seemed very downcast. He looked at me for a moment with his melancholy eyes and said, "Do you know what? I'll tell you something, Shmuel-Aba. There is no justice in Eden."

I looked at him with astonishment. I had no idea what would make Pisherl say such a thing. He sighed. "You know, Shmuel-Aba, I have an uncle, the angel Khaim-Nogid. He has his own house on Elijah-the-Prophet Boulevard. A house with a balcony and a brand new tin roof."

"I know, Pisherl," I replied. "Your uncle is the official liquor dealer of Eden. He's said to be as rich as Korah."

"And a great pig," Pisherl added. "In the Christian Eden, a pig his size would be enough for a huge feast."

"But why are you telling me about him, Pisherl. I'm curious."

"Listen carefully," Pisherl said. "This uncle of mine, this pig, has a goat which gives twenty quarts of milk every twelve minutes. You and I are going to take the goat from its stall and lead it away."

"Where will we take it, Pisherl? Explain yourself. Don't keep me dangling."

"To my uncle Joel, the bookbinder angel, who lives on

Yohanan-the-Cobbler Street. He has tuberculosis and needs the goat's milk more than my uncle the angel Khaim-Nogid does."

"You're right, Pisherl," I agreed. "There really isn't any justice in Eden. The uncle who is rich and healthy as a bear has a goat that gives milk, though he needs it like ten thousand plagues; and the poor uncle, who is sick with tuberculosis and needs the milk to sustain his very life, has a fig for his pains."

Pisherl put his finger to his forehead and thought for a while. (My friend always put a finger to his forehead when he was thinking.) "Shmuel-Aba, do you know what?"

"What, Pisherl?"

"We must steal the goat from my uncle Khaim-Nogid and give it to my uncle the angel Joel."

"Good, Pisherl," I agreed. "But when? Think it over. It has to be done at just the right time."

Pisherl laughed. "It'll be all right, Shmuel-Aba. My uncle Khaim-Nogid takes a nap at noon, and my aunt, the angel Yentl, is away then, being measured for a new pair of wings at the tailor's."

"Well," I said impatiently, "well."

"While she's gone, I'll get the goat out of its stable and lead it to my poor uncle. You'll stand watch in the street, in case my aunt should come back."

"Good, Pisherl. I'm ready. When do you suppose we can pull it off?"

"What do you mean, when?" Pisherl gestured with a wing. "Tomorrow noon, right after lunch."

We agreed on a meeting place. Pisherl described it carefully to me. I went around in a daze for the rest of the day. All night long, I was obsessed by a dream of a goat that gave twenty quarts of milk every twelve minutes.

The next day, precisely at the time arranged, my friend

and I made off quickly for Elijah-the-Prophet Boulevard, where Pisherl's rich uncle lived.

Elijah-the-Prophet Boulevard was very lovely. That's where the *crème de la crème* of Eden lived. The loveliest house belonged to the Zaddik of Saddegura. He cut the same wide swath in Eden as he had on Earth. It's worth mentioning that this was the boulevard on which Rahab the Whore had opened a salon where the richest of the female angels went to have their nails manicured. In Eden, by the way, she had become very pious and read the pious books so that she knew them almost all by heart. As for the manicuring profession, she had very little enthusiasm for it, but a living is a living. In Eden, everyone had almost forgotten that she had once been a whore.

My friend Pisherl and I stationed ourselves before the angel Khaim-Nogid's house and waited for Yentl to leave. When she did, it would be the sign that Pisherl's uncle was taking his nap.

We waited for about half an hour, then Pisherl's aunt, the rich angel's wife, flew out of her house. We looked after her until she disappeared.

"I hope she croaks," Pisherl cursed. "She goes about squandering a fortune in fashion, at the same time as Aunt Rivtsche can't even permit herself the expense of a patch job for her old wings which are so worn through that anyone seeing her thinks she's a beggar and wants to give her alms."

My friend Pisherl wanted to go directly into the courtyard where the goat's stall was, but just at that moment, an old Jew went by, a stout stick in his hand. He stopped my friend and asked, "Where are you going, little angel?"

My friend Pisherl recognized the old fellow at once. It was the prophet Elijah. In the old days, he used to drop down to Earth from time to time to help a poor man or to

It was the prophet Elijah

perform a miracle so that some unlucky fellow might have a little something for his Sabbath. But recent times had turned him bitter. Poor people on Earth had stopped believing in his help and had decided to help themselves. Scornfully, the prophet Elijah had said, "Let them help themselves, those . . . how do they call themselves there? . . . those . . . shoshialists?"

Ever since he had given up his visits to Earth, he went about aimlessly in Eden, strolling down the boulevard that bore his name. He would not have walked down any other street for a king's ransom.

"Where are you going, little angel?"

I was frightened, thinking the whole plan was now ruined. Imagine! Right in the middle of our plot, the prophet Elijah. He always loved to poke his nose into everything. But my friend Pisherl did not lose his head. He knew the old fellow's weakness—to be talked to about the miracles he had accomplished in the days when he was still pleased to perform them. (He can still do them, but he doesn't want to.)

"Let them help themselves . . . the . . . how do they call themselves . . . the shoshialists?" Having said the word *shoshialists,* he spat. Pisherl told him he was right, and went on to tell the old fellow such stories about himself as made the old fellow smile. He took every word that Pisherl said to be the truth. At long last, he took his leave. Pisherl wiped the sweat from his brow.

"Now, Shmuel-Aba," he said, "be careful. Let me know if anyone comes. If they do, God forbid, put your fingers in your mouth and whistle."

"Good," I replied. "But do your best to make it quick, Pisherl."

My friend was gone for some while. Every moment seemed like an eternity. I turned my head to the right and to the left, checking whether, God forbid, anyone was coming. My heart beat crazily.

Pisherl came out leading his uncle's goat on a rope.

"Quickly, Pisherl, quickly. Let's fly to your uncle Joel's. I have a hunch something's going to happen."

"Dope," Pisherl said. "We have to go on foot. A goat hasn't got wings."

We had just taken a few steps when we saw Pisherl's aunt, the rich angel Yentl, flying back in a great hurry. Evidently, she had forgotten something at home. She saw us and immediately raised a hue and cry. My friend and I flew off, making our getaway. The goat dangled in the air, uttering a fearful *meh* over the boulevard.

Pisherl did not let go of the rope. We flew on, panting. Shmaya, the policeman, an angel in a green uniform, who stood at the intersection directing traffic so that the angels, God forbid, would not collide with each other, blew his whistle.

A real chase began. Shmaya, the policeman, still blowing his whistle, was after us. Aunt Yentl, who was a corpulent angel, wheezed like a goose and shouted, "Thieves. Give me back the goat. Woe is me, woe is me. Give me back my goat."

"Pisherl, hold tight to the rope," I cried.

The goat shuddered in mid-air. Its *meh* was deafening.

"Old Elijah delayed us too long," panted my friend, grasping the rope more firmly.

"He shows up most where he's least expected," I said. We flew on.

Our wings were flapping so wildly that I was hardly able to catch my breath. We were young, and our wings were still unworn. We made a number of zigzags. At one moment we thought we had lost our pursuers, but then we heard their wings flapping behind us again.

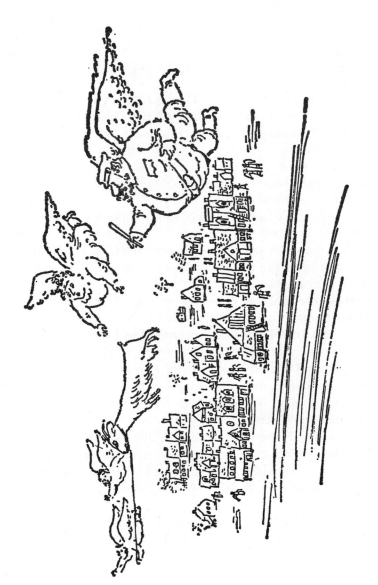

A chase began

The goat was so frightened that its udders opened and the milk began to pour down. Little angels who could not yet fly stood below with open mouths, enjoying every drop that fell!

We arrived at Yohanan-the-Cobbler Street a good bit ahead of our pursuers and alighted. Pisherl knocked at his poverty-stricken uncle's window. His uncle, the angel Joel the bookbinder, came out. He coughed and asked us what was the matter.

"We brought you Uncle Khaim-Nogid's goat. You need it more than he does."

"Who asked you for the favor?" shouted the bookbinder, giving Pisherl two resounding slaps.

At that moment, our pursuers descended. Aunt Yentl was red as a beet. She was shrieking and crying, "The goat. Thieves. Give me back the goat."

Shmaya, the policeman angel in the green uniform, made out a report in which he named us both. Aunt Yentl took the goat by the rope, and promised to fix us properly with Maier-Parakh, the Gemora teacher. She gave the rope a pull and started home with the goat. Saddened and ashamed, my friend and I exchanged looks.

We went home. What Pisherl was thinking, I don't know, but I know that my own heart ached sadly.

For a while, Pisherl kept silent. I did not want to ask him anything. What had happened, had happened. At some point, he lifted his head and, looking at me with his dark, intelligent eyes, he said, "D'you know what, Shmuel-Aba?"

"How should I know?" I answered. "Am I a prophet?"

"I've been thinking," Pisherl said, "that as long as the rich uncles don't permit it, and the poor ones don't want it, there'll be no justice in Eden."

The next day, Pisherl didn't come to Hebrew school.

For a moment, I thought that he hadn't come for fear of being beaten by Maier-Parakh, the Gemora teacher. Later, I learned that it was not fear that kept him from coming to school. Pisherl said he wasn't that kind of a sissy. He had not come because he had been busy helping his father, Shlomo-Zalman, the patch-tailor, pull the basting thread from a hundred pairs of mended wings.

"Pisherl," I said, turning to my friend, "why don't you ever take me home to your house. Are you ashamed of me, perhaps?"

"God forbid!" said Pisherl in a frightened voice. "That's stupid, Shmuel-Aba. You're welcome to come home with me right this minute, if you like."

We both flew off to Pisherl's house. Pisherl's father, Shlomo-Zalman, was an angel with a large Adam's apple and protruding eyes. He lived not far from the meadow on which was pastured the Messiah-Ox.

The Messiah-Ox is huge and fat. Nobody knows how much it weighs because there isn't a scale in Eden large enough to weigh it without breaking. On its right side, the Messiah-Ox has a huge brown spot that looks like the map of Eden.

When we came to Shlomo-Zalman's house, we found the angel Gabriel standing before a large mirror. Shlomo-Zalman was engaged in fitting the wings that Gabriel was leaving with him for repairs.

The angel Gabriel is a tall, thick-set angel. He is very rich, but also very stingy. In all his life, he has never had a new pair of wings made. He keeps having his first wings continually repaired.

"Here . . . here . . . on the right side . . . it's a bit . . ." the angel Gabriel was saying. "Right here, Shlomo-Zalman."

Shlomo-Zalman, the patch-tailor, made some marks with

his chalk, some measurements with his tape measure. He jumped about, continually uttering reassurances. "It will be all right, I promise you, Reb Gabriel. It will be all right. Depend on it. You can count on Shlomo-Zalman."

But the angel Gabriel did not like to count on anyone. He lifted his shoulders, finding a fault here and a fault there. For Shlomo-Zalman, it was extremely painful.

Gabriel bothered the patch-tailor for a good hour. Then he left. At the door he stopped and said one last time, "Remember, Shlomo-Zalman, I need the wings by Passover. Remember." No sooner was the angel Gabriel gone than Pisherl's father became quite another person. He danced about, singing,

> What shall we eat at the Great Feast?
> The Messiah-Ox and Leviathan.
> The Messiah-Ox and Leviathan
> Is what we'll eat at the Great Feast.

At the sewing machine, there sat the apprentice angel Siomkeh. He was running up wing seams and humming softly. The apprentice angel Berl stood at the pressing table. He was continually testing the iron with a finger to see if it was hot enough.

Siomkeh and Berl, the two apprentices, had once been close friends, almost one body and one soul; but from the time that they had both fallen in love with Roisl, the Eden grocer's young daughter, they were at sword's points, continually provoking and making life miserable for each other.

Roisl, Israel-Mosheh's daughter, was a young and lovely angel who made fools of both the young apprentices. She would lead one on, and then the other. One day, they all but killed each other, these two former friends. They threw the pressing irons at each other's heads and, for the next several weeks, came to work with bandaged heads.

Siomkeh had already tried suicide. He had hung himself from his suspenders but had completely forgotten that an Eden angel cannot die. After some twenty-four hours of dangling in mid-air, he had untied his suspenders and cursed Eden and the apprentice Berl. He would have cursed the source of all his woes, that is, the Eden grocer's daughter, had his heart permitted it.

I was delighted with Pisherl's home. There was a large room, an alcove and a kitchen—and that was it, the entire house. In the big room they worked, and in the alcove they slept; Pisherl's mother, Hannah-Deborah, busied herself all day in the kitchen cooking lunch and supper for the entire household.

The window was open. We could see the Eden meadow where the Messiah-Ox was grazing. Three barefooted little angels herded it, to keep it from getting into anybody's garden. One of them was playing "Mosheh the Cowherd" on his pipe and the other two were singing.

At evening time, the two apprentices stuck their needles into their lapels, and went away to dream about their mutual beloved. Pisherl's father went to the tailor's synagogue for evening prayers. Pisherl and I stood before the open window, watching the evening darken over the Eden meadow. We could hear the silver Eden crickets chirping. The Messiah-Ox was cropping the grass. I admired his appetite.

The three cowherds were singing. That is, one of them played on his pipe while the two others sang. Whoever has not heard the singing of the Eden cowherds has no inkling in the world what loveliness is.

> The Messiah-Ox we've guarded
> Ever since the early dawn;

Guarded him at his huge grazing
Till the day is almost done.

Pipes a bird his song in Eden,
Then his whistling's full of joy;
When a calf springs on the meadow,
Then his springing's full of joy.

Crickets chirping in the grasses
Trill, trill, trill and trill, trill, trill;
And the wind, that ancient prankster,
Turns the vanes of the windmill.

Yearning and sweet, the piping faded away. All we could see of the cowherds were their silhouettes. We could hear the Messiah-Ox chewing its cud. The moon went up through the trees. I touched my friend Pisherl who stood thoughtfully silent. "Pisherl, you know what?"

"What, Shmuel-Aba?"

"Let's take a little stroll."

"Where, Shmuel-Aba?"

"I thought we might wander a little in the Three Patriarchs' Allée."

"All right."

We spread our wings and flew. Pisherl breathed deeply of the Eden breeze.

"Your father's a fine angel, Pisherl. He works so hard, and yet he appears to be very poor."

Pisherl made no reply. He hated talking about his father's poverty.

The Three Patriarchs' Allée was crowded with young couples. Many were flying about. Some sat on benches, whispering, though we did not understand why; it pleased us, nevertheless. We promised each other that when we grew up, each of us would find a female angel with whom we, too, would whisper in the Three Patriarchs' Allée.

We heard a deep, doleful sigh. We looked about, wondering who it was. Soon, we recognized the tailor's apprentice, the angel Siomkeh, who was walking alone in the Allée.

From the other side of the Allée, another sigh was heard. It was the angel Berl. He too could find no rest. "When we grow up and become adults," Pisherl said, "we too will sigh."

"Even more deeply than the two tailor's apprentices," I added.

"Certainly," Pisherl agreed. We alighted, directly in the middle of the Allée. We walked back and forth, eavesdropping on the whisperers, who could be heard among the trees. One angel was swearing eternal faith. His beloved did not believe him. He threatened to throw himself down to Earth.

"What are you doing here, Pisherl? Come home." We recognized Pisherl's sister Ettl. She was strolling in the Allée with one of her girlfriends.

"I don't want to go home. I want to walk about a little longer with my friend Shmuel-Aba," Pisherl replied.

His sister went on. My friend and I looked at each other. "Your sister is pretty," I said. "Her wings are so rosy."

"She is betrothed," Pisherl said proudly. "The wedding is set for the Saturday after Shavuoth."

"Will you invite me to the wedding, Pisherl?"

"Of course," my friend promised. Then we separated until the next morning.

All night long, I dreamed of a wedding. Pisherl was the father-in-law and I was the groom. Musicians played. The bride wept.

I started from my sleep and realized it was only a dream. I had a sharp pang of regret for its loveliness.

V

~~~

Ghosts in Eden

&HE NARRATION had tired me a little. I rested for a while, then looked at my listeners. I wanted to see if they had fallen asleep as I told of my adventures in Paradise; but I saw the rabbi clutching his beard and the rich man with his hands folded over his belly, while the rabbinical judge sat with his mouth wide open, as though warding off an evil eye, and I understood that I could go on with my story.

I woke from my strange dream about midnight. In the dream, as you know, I was the groom, my friend Pisherl was the father-in-law, and Pisherl's sister Ettl was the bride. I tried to go back to sleep so that I might spin out my lovely dream a little longer, but I couldn't. The lovely dream was far, far away, on the other side of the mills of Paradise.

Barefoot, and in a nightgown, I left my bed and went to the window. The street was drenched in moon-silver. Even in Eden, such a bright moonlit night was a rarity. I opened the window and breathed in the mild midnight

61

breeze, then breathed it out again, together with a greeting to my friend Pisherl and to his rosy-winged, pretty sister.

Opposite me, on the sidewalk, two shadows collided. They spat, then stood wondering. The first spoke. "Is it you, Siomkeh?"

"Is it you, Berl?"

"What are you doing in the street so late at night, Siomkeh?"

"And what are you doing, Berl?"

I recognized the two infatuated angels who worked for Pisherl's father, Shlomo-Zalman the patch-tailor. I strained both ears. It would have been a pity to lose a syllable of their conversation. "I can't fall asleep, Siomkeh. Every time I close my eyes, I see the Eden grocer's daughter."

"It's the same with me, Berl," sighed Siomkeh. "I can't endure it."

They stood for a while, silent. I could see the needles glittering in their lapels. Siomkeh said, "I envy the humblest tailor lad on Earth. If he's unlucky in love, he can at least take poison or drown himself in the river."

"We have no choice," replied the angel Berl. "We have to endure our misfortune forever. A miserable word, *forever*. Who invented it, and why?" I watched the two questions "who" and "why" flutter from the angel Berl's lips and remain suspended in the Eden atmosphere that was filled now with the sweet light of the moon. They separated—Siomkeh to the right and Berl to the left. I pitied the two unhappy angels and their wandering through the nights of Eden. Deeply, deeply pitied them.

I thought of the Eden grocer's daughter, the source of their unrest. No doubt she was fast asleep, her hair disheveled on her pillow. Her wings, with which she had covered herself, had slipped down from her body. Perhaps she was smiling in her dream and did not even know of the misfortune she had provoked—a misfortune that could find no rest, but longed for death, and could not die. "In Eden," I thought, "a moonlit night also has its ghosts."

At that moment, I did not know that on this very night it would be my fate to see and to hear much more than the sighs of the unfortunate tailor's apprentices.

I heard a sharp and desperate cry. Lifting my head, I saw the angel Shimon-Ber for the first time. He was, as he almost always was, dead drunk, and was leading two unborn children by the hand. They kept tearing themselves away, shrieking and crying.

"You shut your traps, you bastards," Shimon-Ber said furiously. "Will you shut up, or no?" His red beard was in disorder. He was so drunk that his eyes rolled in his head.

The two children cried, "We don't want to be born. Have pity, Shimon-Ber. We don't want to go down to Earth." One of the children was a girl, the other, a boy. Shimon-Ber had been ordered to set them down on Earth tonight, where they were to be born as twins.

"I don't want to be born," Shimon-Ber mimicked. "Who asked you, you bastards?" The little boy, whom Shimon-Ber was leading by the right hand, hit upon an idea.

To the drunken angel, he said, "Reb Shimon-Ber. Let go of my hand for a moment. I want to wipe my nose." For an instant, Shimon-Ber was off his guard and let the boy's hand go. The little fellow ran off. Then, on that moonlit Eden night, a real chase began.

Shimon-Ber flapped his coarse, cottony wings and pursued the little angel, holding the little girl firmly by the hand as he dragged her along with him.

I saw it all with my own eyes. My heart trembled and I prayed to the Creator of the world that he should perform a miracle so that Shimon-Ber would not catch the runaway

I recognized the two infatuated angels

child. Evidently, my prayer did not help. Shimon-Ber caught him, grasped him by an ear, and dragged him off. "Just you wait till we get to the border. You'll get a real snap on your nose—bastards."

The poor little girl angel was entirely guiltless, but when Shimon-Ber is angry, it's all the same to him, guilty or not. He must and will vent his wrath. I saw him dragging her by the hand and the boy by the ears. They flew off in the direction of the border. I watched them until they were entirely gone.

I thought of the fate of the unborn children, and tried to feel their fear of Earth, but I was as yet too young and too small to understand it. "Tomorrow, I'll tell my friend Pisherl everything I've experienced tonight. It'll be interesting to hear what he says." I would say, "I know that Shimon-Ber is a bandit and a drunkard, and I've heard a great deal else about him; yesterday I saw it all for myself. It's all true, what they say about that scoundrel. But tell me, Pisherl, why do the children shudder so at the prospect of being born and why are they so frightened of the Earth?"

I tried to imagine what Pisherl's reply would be. I even put my finger to my forehead, as my friend did, thinking that the finger would help me in some way. And yet, somehow, it all remained as perplexing as before. I could not find any answer by myself.

I heard the sound of beating wings. Looking up, I saw the glittering of fires at a great distance; many, many little fires. They kept coming closer; the beating of wings became stronger, swifter.

I was astonished. I had never, until then, heard such a beating of wings. "Who can it be?" I thought, straining my eyes. I saw an angel with huge black wings. He had a thousand eyes that flickered, threatening and red, through the white moonlit night. In his hand, the angel with the black wings carried a sword. "It's the Angel of Death," I realized. "No doubt, he's flying down to Earth. Here in Eden, no one is afraid of him, but there, on Earth, they tremble before him. No sooner do they hear the flapping of his wings, then they are overcome with fear. Jews run to the synagogue to recite psalms; their wives hurry to wail at the graveyards, to ward him off. But it's said that nothing helps. Whom the Angel of Death must take, he takes. No amount of weeping or praying can help.

The angel with the black wings came closer and closer. He waved his huge sword about, making it clear that he was flying on serious business . . . a very, very serious mission.

A star detached itself from the Eden sky. It flew to greet the angel with the black wings and detained him. "Angel of Death, where are you flying?" asked the star, shuddering. I could not tell whether it shuddered for fear or for pity.

The black-winged Angel of Death answered, "I'm flying down to Earth where I'm supposed to gather the soul of a bride and bring it to the throne of God." My heart began to throb. "The soul of a bride," I thought. "Pisherl's sister is a bride." Then I remembered that the Eden brides had nothing to fear from the Angel of Death, and I felt reassured.

The star trembled and shook and pleaded. "Turn back, angel with the black wings. What do you want with the poor earthly bride? Have pity on her. Let her delight in her flowers, her love, and her dreams."

"Ah—a new pleader for justice," said the Angel of Death angrily. "Who asked you for your pity? Your duty is to shine; then shine away in good health, and don't mind other people's business."

But the star would not let up. He began to argue with the black angel, trying to persuade him: "That earthly bride is not my sister; she isn't even a relative. It's only that I saw her eyes once when she turned them up. It's only that I heard a sigh of hers once . . . a murmur. She was wishing on me, asking me to send her love to her betrothed."

"Why are you telling me this?" the black winged angel asked sternly. "Do you mind not standing in my way? I'd cut a fine figure, indeed, if I were to be as sentimental as you are."

The star all but sobbed. It pleaded with tears in its eyes and trembled all over. "Have you no pity for a life so young? Only nineteen years old altogether. Think a bit. Nineteen years old."

"You're something of a poet, I see," said the angel scornfully. "But it would be a lot better for you if you forbore to disturb my work."

"You're a brute and a murderer," said the star sadly. "You have a heart of stone. You aren't moved by any plea. But just remember what I tell you. . . ."

"What is there for me to remember?"

"Remember," said the star piously, "remember what is written in the Passover song about the kid . . ."

"And what does it say there?" asked the Angel of Death, ironically.

"In the song about the kid, it is written that in the end, the Lord of the Universe will come and he will slay the Angel of Death."

I saw the Angel of Death tremble. The star had reminded him of his own end. It was a remarkable shudder: the fear of death, for himself.

I was curious to know how all of this would end. Would the angel with the black wings turn back? Would the earthly bride open her eyes tomorrow morning, as always? Would she rejoice in the sun, in her flowers, in her loved one?

Evidently not. The Angel of Death whirled his sword about. Sparks all but flew from it. He spread his huge black wings and flew on.

"You're going . . ." called the star in a broken voice.

"I must," the angel answered harshly. Without further ado, he disappeared.

I could still see his gleaming eyes in the distance; I could still hear the sound of his beating wings. The star fell somewhere into the Eden grass and sought consolation among the crickets.

Strange thoughts entered my head. In the same moonlit night, I had heard the cries of children who did not want to be born; and the harsh, firm "I must" of the angel with the thousand eyes who was flying down to Earth to extinguish a life.

Opposite my window a cherry tree was blooming. Though its crown was bathed in moonlight, it cast a shadow on the Earth. I watched the shadow and saw how it trembled. I asked myself, "Must a shadow tremble, too? But for whom? Perhaps for itself?" For the first time since I had been in Eden, I was frightened of shadows and of spirits. I tried to reassure myself. I talked aloud so I could hear myself better. "Fool," I scolded. "What are you afraid of? And of whom are you afraid? Shimon-Ber didn't have you in mind. It wasn't you he was leading down to Earth to be born; and it wasn't you that the angel with the thousand eyes flew down to uproot from the Earth." In the crown of the cherry tree, a wind murmured in its sleep. The shadow of the tree on the ground was trying to catch its own tail, without success.

"Maybe I ought to leave the window?" I thought. Nevertheless, I continued to stand there without budging from the spot. My heart told me that this night in Eden had further ghosts for me. They would reveal themselves in due time.

I heard singing. Softly and sadly the melody sounded through the moonlit Eden night. I listened carefully, trying to discover where it came from, but no matter how hard I tried, I was unable to find its source. The music approached my street, and at last I could see the figure that drew a melody across the moonlit Eden streets.

It was Crazy Pearl, the angel who had lost her mind because of an unfortunate love affair. Pisherl had told me that she, Pearl, had had an affair with the Eden bookkeeper Getsl. Getsl keeps track of the good deeds that Jews do. At the end of every year, he adds them up and turns the sum over to the angel Michael. For three years, Pearl went about with the Eden bookkeeper, who swore her an eternal love. Pearl thought that everything he said was God's own truth. She, that good pious soul, did not know that there are charlatans in Eden who will play with a young girl's heart for a while, only to throw it away later.

Pearl worked for an Eden milliner. Every *groschen* that she earned, she put away, depriving herself of necessities, waiting for the happy day when she would be married to the Eden bookkeeper. Then, the little hoard she had saved throughout her years of drudgery would be very useful. In the end, all of her expectations collapsed. Her lover discarded her and married the angel Michael's youngest daughter, Eve.

Pearl wept her nights away. She would not eat or sleep. No sort of consolation was any help to her. One fine day, she went out, her hair disordered, her wings in disarray. She set up a terrible din, throwing herself at passers-by, until she had to be restrained. Two angels dragged her over to the rain faucet and splashed cold water on her until at last she calmed down. From that time on, she was silent, saying not a word to anyone. Whenever she saw an angel, she avoided him. She spent entire days in her house. If anyone spoke to her, she did not reply, and, though she looked calmly into his eyes, she understood nothing.

On moonlit nights (my friend Pisherl told me), when all the angels are asleep, Pearl leaves her house. She walks about the streets singing her love songs.

On this moonlit night, I watched her. She was a tall angel with glittering eyes. Her hair lay scattered over her shoulders; her wings were disordered. Her disheveled head lifted to the stars, she sang:

> Once as I went strolling
> Through barley fields and wheat,
> I lost my dearest lover,
> Lost him through deceit.
>
> Between a yes and no, I lost
> My darling lover dear.
> Perhaps it's true, you little birds,
> You've seen my love somewhere?
>
> If yes, then tell him, little birds,
> That I still sit and wait;
> If yes, then ask him, little birds,
> What prompted his deceit?

I swear that I saw tears in her eyes. The wind played in her tangled hair, disordering it even more. It seemed to me that the wind made fun of the crazy angel, and I was deeply grieved.

Pearl passed near my window. She paused awhile and sighed deeply. Surely, she could sense that there was some- one nearby who sympathized with her pain. I wanted to say something to her; I wanted to tell her that she ought to say, "To Hell with Getsl the bookkeeper"; I wanted to tell

Pearl sang

her that that charlatan wasn't worth a single tear of her
lovely eyes. But I said nothing. To this moment, I don't
know why I kept silent. Perhaps if I had said a few decent
words to her then, I might have consoled her. And it may
be that I kept still because even in Eden, the kinds of
words necessary to heal the wounds of unhappy love are
not to be found.

Pearl went on her way. Todress, the south wind, and
Shmelke, the east wind, those two Eden pranksters, played
with her hair.

I could remain at the window no longer. I was so drawn
to the crazy angel that, dressed as I was, in my nightshirt, I
followed her. I walked barefooted over the cool silver
moonbeams that rolled about so bountifully on the streets
of Eden.

Pearl went before me; I followed her. She had no idea I
was there but walked on slowly, singing

> The moon at midnight brightly shines,
> The angels all sleep soundly;
> But, oh what grief, dear mother,
> What dreadful grief has found me.
>
> A love, a love, a love affair
> With a handsome angel.
> In the crown of Eden, he
> Was the fairest jewel.
>
> He hugged and kissed and toyed with me,
> His promises were splendid.
> He called me "sweetheart," "crown of gold,"
> Then suddenly, it ended.
>
> Oh fair young angels, hear my song,
> It's full of pain and sorrow;
> False angels who are true today
> Will be untrue tomorrow.

Pearl's song disturbed me terribly. I watched her approaching the King David Wood and followed her.

Todress the south wind and Shmelke the east wind played with my nightshirt, lifting it over my head. I begged them to leave me alone; this was no time for such fun. Some other time, if they liked, I'd be more than ready for them. The two pranksters whispered, one in my right, the other in my left ear, "Better a game with your shirt than a game at love, Shmuel-Aba. The shirt game produces no such sorrows as the game of love. Believe us, it's better. Come on, let's play with your shirt."

I drove them away, scolding them harshly, telling them that I was not always in the mood to be teased.

Near the wood, Pearl stopped. She spread her arms out and sang into the wood—

> It was here, in this wood,
> On a moonlit night
> That my love
> Was sacrificed.

I stood still, my hands folded, and listened to her singing. Her song sounded like a prayer and a memorial service at once.

> Ask the tree in the forest,
> Ask the wind in the field
> Why you have darkened
> My bright, bright world.

"Yes," I thought, "you may ask for a year and a day for all the answer you'll get."

> Ask the bird in the tree,
> Ask the river fish
> If ever they lost
> A realm half so rich.

Pearl went into the King David Wood. I followed her no farther. To tell the truth, I was scared. Her madness and the dark forest frightened me. I stood, as if frozen, at the entrance to the wood. I did not myself know whether I had dreamed all this, or whether it was true.

I spread my wings. The morning dew glistened on them. I flew home, thinking that there I would forget the nightmares and the ghosts of Eden that had shown themselves to me on this moonlit night.

But I could not forget. To this very day, the ghosts of Eden stand before my eyes. The two infatuated apprentice angels yearning for death; the children who did not want to be born; the prayer of the star pleading with the Angel of Death not to uproot the trembling earthly life of a bride; and, most of all, the singing insanity of a disastrous Eden love affair.

The rabbi shook himself, and started as if out of a daze. "Eh . . . what's that, scamp? What'd you say?"

The rich man drummed his fingers on his belly. No doubt, he was trying to say the German word *sonderbar* and was not able to.

The rabbinical judge, who had been sitting the entire time with his mouth open, shut it now, swallowing a dozen flies that had, during my narrative, crept into his mouth.

My mother wiped away the tear that had been trembling in her right eye.

My father drummed the table with his fingers. I did not understand what he meant by the gesture.

I felt that I could tell no more of my story that night. I excused myself, and went off without supper to lie down in my cradle. I heard the rabbi, the rabbinical judge and the rich man saying their good-by's to my father; I heard them kiss the *mezuzah*.

As if to no one in particular, the rabbi said, "Then it would seem that tomorrow night, God willing, he'll go on with his story, Faivl."

I fell asleep.

VI

In King David's Estates

THE NEXT NIGHT when the rabbi, the rabbinical judge, and the rich man were again at our table waiting for me to go on with my narrative, I watched them for a while. They were pale and had slept insufficiently. The rabbi's beard, or so it seemed to me, was whiter by a hair. Evidently the stories of the Eden ghosts had severely disturbed him.

"Well," my father muttered, "well. Tell on. You can see they're waiting to hear you, and yet you just sit there like a clod."

When she heard the word *clod,* my mother, who was standing at the door, was instantly ready to come to my defense . . . to tell my father what's what; but this time I wouldn't let her. One look from me, and she stayed rooted to the spot. My father, who was already trembling before the storm, calmed down, and I resumed my story.

After all the sights I had seen on that white moonlit night, I was unable to think of sleep. I waited with difficulty until it was dawn in Eden; then I flew quickly to my friend Pisherl's house. I knocked at his window. Pisherl was still asleep. He did not hear my tapping. I knocked harder—so hard that my fingers hurt. At long last, I woke him.

"Pisherl, come. Hurry, quickly."

"What's the matter, Shmuel-Aba?" my friend inquired, rubbing his eyes.

"Come on out. You'll soon know." My whole body was trembling. My friend came out.

Taking him by the hand, I looked into his sleepy eyes and said, "Let's fly to the King David Wood."

We flew. On the way, I told him about all the nightmares that had appeared to me. Pisherl sighed. My story made a deep impression on him. Giving his wings a shake, he said, "I've never yet seen such things as you tell me of, Shmuel-Aba. I've heard a great deal, but I've seen nothing. It seems one sees such things only on sleepless nights. You were lucky to have had a sleepless night. I envy you, Shmuel-Aba."

I couldn't understand him. His words seemed strange. What was there to be envious of? When I said as much to him, he looked at me with a strangely distant look. "Whatever the day hides or blinds with its sunlight, the night reveals. It lifts the veil of things and you get to look into the abyss. It's a pity I slept through such an eventful night."

We flew on. The early sunlight warmed our wings. The Eden wind was young and fresh. He played with our hair prankishly, wondering at his own temerity. When we approached the King David Wood, the wind left us, springing quickly in among the trees to tell the Eden rabbits that guests were coming of whom they need not be afraid. The two "flyers" had not brought bows and arrows along.

My friend and I let ourselves down near the entrance to the wood.

"Right here," I said, pointing, "right here is where the crazy angel Pearl disappeared into the wood. I was afraid to follow her. Come, Pisherl. Maybe we can still find her." We went into the wood and looked for tracks of the crazy one but found none. Birds were twittering in the trees. Dew glistened on the grass in large silver drops.

"Perhaps the drops are tears unfortunate love has wept on the grass," I said to my friend.

"It may be," Pisherl whispered. We stopped before a large, wild, dew-filled Eden rose. With awe and piety, we recited a chapter of the psalms, but the tears remained.

"What happened to Pearl's tracks?" I asked my friend.

"No doubt the Eden streetsweeper swept them away. That's the way things are done in Eden. The day isn't supposed to know that often the nights are filled with nonsense and madness."

"Then it's useless to search. Let's turn back, Pisherl."

Pisherl was lost in thought. His finger was at his forehead. I stood by and waited to see what he would think up.

A bird flew over Pisherl's head and whistled, "Pee. Pee." All the birds knew my friend Pisherl. They were fond of him and often greeted him. In bird language, "Pee. Pee" means "Pisherl."

"We won't go to Hebrew school today," Pisherl said finally.

"But what of the Gemora teacher, Maier-Parakh? He'll beat the daylights out of us tomorrow."

"To Hell with him," said my friend with a wave of his hand.

"Agreed," I said. "To Hell with him. The monster."

We lingered a bit longer, listening to the birds sing, breathing deeply the smell of the grass.

"Come, Shmuel-Aba."

"Where, Pisherl?"

"We'll fly to King David's estates."

"To King David's estates? Will they let us in?"

"I have a friend there. A shepherd angel named Laibl. I haven't seem him in a month of Sundays."

"Is it far from here, Pisherl?"

"A couple of hours' flight to the east. Our King David is terribly rich. He goes about all day with a golden crown on his head, his hands clasped behind his back, watching the angels at work sowing his fields. He dearly loves to hear his psalms being sung. He thinks his songs are the most beautiful in the world, and the angels who work for him are obliged to sing them as they work."

"Good, Pisherl. We'll fly there and listen to the angels singing King David's psalms."

We spread our wings and started. Our flight lay toward the east. The sun dazzled our eyes. For the first half hour, it was difficult flying into the sun. Then we got used to it. I was already burning with curiosity to see the estates of King David.

My friend pointed down with his finger. "Shmuel-Aba, do you see?"

I looked and saw green fields stretching far out toward the horizon. On the right hand, there were huge verdant forests; on the left, a river that looked like a silver belt the Queen of Sheba might have lost. I could not contain myself and cried out, "Oh . . . how lovely."

We dropped down a bit in order to see better. In the fields stood the peasant angels, their long shirts out of their trousers. They were plowing and sowing. Huge drops of sweat dripped from their foreheads. The angels sang:

> When dawn lights up the windows,
> We're driven out of doors,

Out of our dingy corners,
Out of the shabby house.

Cuckoo, cuckoo, you're a witness
To all that we endure;
Tell our woe to blessed God;
Take Him our silent tear.

Tell Him that we plow the fields,
And take the harvest in,
And tell him that our children starve,
At night, when we come home.

Cuckoo, cuckoo, you're a witness
To all that we endure;
Tell our woe to blessed God;
Take Him our silent tear.

"Why are their songs so sad?" I asked.

"Why? Is that your question?" My friend sighed. "Just look at the lives they lead, and you won't need to ask. May those who envy them be condemned to live as they do." He pointed. I looked down and saw small low huts of clay with straw-thatched roofs. "There, in those huts. That's where the poor angels live. They never get enough to eat; they never dream a dream to its end."

"Why is their fate so dismal, Pisherl?"

"Why? You ask 'why'?" Pisherl gritted his teeth. "Because there is no justice in heaven. In appearance, they are angels just like all the others. They have wings; they sing psalms. Just the same—look at them."

A tear fell from Pisherl's eyes. I caught it in my hand. It was hot.

"I gather, then, that Eden isn't Eden for everyone?" I inquired.

"For the time being, no," my friend answered. And we flew on.

"And this is all happening in King David's estates," I thought. Aloud, I said, "Where's the justice in it?"

Pisherl turned. "Fool. Don't you remember what the patriarch Abraham said on that Sabbath walk? 'Justice shmustice.' "

I remembered the conversation of the patriarchs and I turned red with shame. "Well, what about King David?" I inquired. "What does King David do?"

"If only all the angels could live like him. He carries on in Eden as God would in France. He goes around all day with nothing to do. Or else he plays on his harp, or he dallies with Abishag; and when he gets bored he bothers the pretty daughters of the poor angels."

"He hasn't forgotten his old tricks?"

"No. On the contrary. In Eden he can really do them. After all . . . King David!"

We flew over the silver Eden river. Barefooted women angels were standing at the river's edge washing clothes. One of them, a young angel with red, swollen hands, was singing:

> Well for you Zaddikim,
> Oh, it's well for you.
> At the Eden stream,
> We wash your clothes for you.
>
> And what you have made dirty,
> We can wash it here,
> And what you have bespattered,
> We will make it fair.

The other angels, old as well as young, who were standing bent over at the water's edge, replied in chorus:

> Praise to the Creator
> Who rules the world His way,

Who set the whole Creation
In a just array.

Of one, he made a harpist,
Another washes clothes,
While still another labors
Sweating in the fields.

From the clay huts there could be heard the sounds of infants. They lay alone in their cribs, crying their hearts out. Braina, the Eden wet nurse, an angel with huge, full breasts, went from hut to hut nursing the little angels. The lord of the estates had hired her for this purpose so that the darlings wouldn't keep their mothers from their work.

"Where does Braina get the milk to nurse so many of the little angels?" I asked my friend.

"How come you don't understand, dummy?" grumbled Pisherl. "She waters it."

We flew on, turning now to the right toward the gardens. The sun was growing hot. We looked for a shady corner. In the midst of a luxuriant park, there stood a marble palace. The windows of the palace were wide open. Two young female angels, with down clinging to their hair, were airing out the bedclothes.

Pisherl said, "That's the palace of King David. It has more than a hundred rooms. King David, his wives, and his mistresses live there."

Awed, I said, "A lovely palace. It would be worth taking a look at what goes on there."

"God forbid," cried Pisherl. "No sooner across the threshold and you'd be caught by the eunuchs and forced to become a page."

"A page in King David's household! Can that be so bad, Pisherl?"

"Wish it on your worst enemy, Shmuel-Aba. You simply don't know what you're talking about. That's all you need—to stand around all day, holding King David's train or tickling the soles of his feet."

I shuddered to the tips of my wings. I imagined a couple of sweaty feet with huge corns on the toes. It was my job to tickle them. The sweat was suffocating; King David was continually angry, shouting, "Harder, harder. Tickle harder, Shmuel-Aba. What are you? A page or a clod?" Brrr . . . I shuddered again.

We could hear the sound of a harp. Pisherl pricked up his ears. "Do you hear, Shmuel-Aba?"

"I hear, Pisherl."

"King David is playing his harp. Let's fly, but on wing tips, silently, so he won't hear us."

We flew toward the sound of the music. Under a shady oak, King David sat. He was playing the harp. Near him sat a young girl with black, wavy hair and a raspberry birthmark on her left cheek. My friend and I settled down near the couple. I looked at King David. He was a man of middle height, corpulent, with sharp green eyes. His little beard was reddish, cut somewhat close.

"He's the one who wrote the psalms?" I asked my friend in a whisper.

My friend put his finger to his mouth, "Shhhh . . ." I understood. Now it was best to be silent and to listen. It must be said that King David played quite well. The girl beside him grew lovelier as he played. When he finished, I saw an eagle circling over his head. There was the sound of a thousand voices from the trees in the garden. "King David of Israel, long life to you."

The king smiled. He seemed pleased. The girl stood up.

"Where are you off to in such a hurry, Shulamith? Why is it you're so pressed for time?" said the king, taking her by the hand.

In the midst of a luxuriant park
there stood a marble palace

"I must go, father-in-law. Solomon may be looking for me already in the vineyard. You know, if I'm even a little bit late, he starts looking for me. By now, he's sung the 'Song of Songs' a dozen times."

But King David would not let her go. He pulled her down to him under the shady tree and embraced her. "Dear Shulamith . . . little dove . . . kitten . . ." Shulamith tore herself from his arms. Her hair tumbled down; her face was aglow.

"Leave me in peace, father-in-law," she breathed excitedly. "It's a sin. You're blaspheming against your psalms."

"If you want me to, kitten," whispered King David, "I'll write even better psalms for you. Another 'Song of Songs,' like Solomon's . . . only more beautiful . . ." We heard the sound of a kiss, then of another, then a third. Shulamith pleaded, tearing herself from his arms. "Let go, I beg you. Let me go, father-in-law! Solomon will find out. There'll be a scandal."

"He'll find out nothing, kitten. Like hell he'll find out, my dove . . ."

"The birds will tell him, father-in-law. Solomon understands the language of the birds."

"The birds in my estates," the king was panting, "will tell him nothing. The birds in my estates are loyal to *me*."

Again we heard a kiss, a second, a third. Who knows where it all would have led, had not King David heard Bathsheba calling, "David. Where are you, David?"

Shulamith started to her feet, patted her hair, and, quick as a doe, aroused and inflamed as she was, she was gone. King David rose, took his harp, and started off in the direction of the marble palace. We watched him go until he disappeared among the trees.

From the fields there came the song of the laboring angels. It had the aura of raisins and almonds, of sweat and psalms. I looked at my friend. He looked at me. We understood each other.

"What if Bathsheba knew what just happened here?" I said.

"Bathsheba is used to such goings-on, but if Abishag were to find out . . . don't even ask what would happen."

"Well, what about King Solomon? What if *he* knew? Would he be silent?"

"He'd tear the entire 'Song of Songs' up in his rage. It would be better if he didn't find out. It would be a pity to lose the 'Song of Songs.' "

"No skin off my nose. Let them tear hell out of each other."

We wiped the dust from our wings and took to the air. The sun was already low on the horizon.

"Now we'll go find Laibl the shepherd angel. He's an old friend of mine. I haven't seen him in the longest time."

"Where will we find him, Pisherl?"

"Come, I know just where. You see that green hill. That's where the sheep are pastured." A dog began to bark. I was frightened and clutched my friend Pisherl's wings. "Don't be afraid, you little dope," he said, reassuring me. "It's Laibl's dog. His name is Sheftl. He's a Jewish dog. He only barks, never bites."

We flew nearer to the low hill. Before we descended, we paused, listening to Laibl's piping.

I looked closely at the shepherd angel Laibl. He pleased me a lot. He was a blond angel with bright blue eyes.

"Now there's the true King David," I whispered. "That's exactly how King David ought to look: barefooted, handsome, playing beautifully on his pipe."

Pisherl looked at me. "You're dreaming, Shmuel-Aba.

That's Laibl, the shepherd, playing on his pipe; the one with the crown on his head was King David."

"But King David was also a shepherd."

Pisherl did not reply. He was lost in thought, gazing at the little silver clouds floating about in the Eden heaven. When they collided, they made thin, silver sounds, then they drifted off on their separate ways.

The shepherd angel Laibl put his pipe away in the grass. He sang sweetly, sincerely. I shivered with delight.

> Between the prayers of evening,
> The flutist plays better;
> Between the prayers of evening
> Sorrows turn sweeter.
>
> The clouds become then
> So dear, and so far,
> They offer your longing
> Up to a star.
>
> Then woe to the longing,
> The yearning that's mute,
> And woe to the grief
> That finds not its flute.

My eyes began to fill with tears. My friend Pisherl all but cried aloud. We settled to the ground. The angel Laibl ran up to my friend; they kissed each other. Sheftl, the dog, barked in welcome.

Pisherl introduced me to his friend Laibl, the shepherd angel. "Laibl, this is my new friend. His name is Shmuel-Aba. He's a good fellow."

We all sat down. Sheftl quit barking. He had become my friend too. He lay down near me and began to catch Eden flies.

It began to grow dark in King David's estates. We all kept quiet as we watched the shadows taking over the

The angel Luibl sat playing on a pipe

fields, section by section, creeping closer. They were almost on Laibl's sheep.

Pisherl sat down next to the shepherd. "Laibl, sing me the song you sang me a year ago when I visited you."

Laibl's blue eyes turned a shade darker. It was as if the deepening evening had drawn itself into his eyes. He sang:

> The horses of evening
> Are led to their harness
> While all of the earth
> Is shading to darkness.
>
> Pipe, shepherd, pipe
> Your song of the evening;
> You make the stars bright,
> You make the birds weary.
>
> The sheep in the meadow
> Long to go home;
> Your clay hut is warm
> With the warmth of a dream.

The angel Laibl bent his head. We were all silent. The crickets in the grass and the frogs in the swamp were saying their evening prayers. Laibl got up and called the flock together with his pipe. "The flock has to be driven home," he told us. "You wait for me; I'll be right back. We'll spend the night together. A night in King David's estates can be extremely interesting. There's plenty to see and hear."

Laibl began to drive the flock home. We looked after him. His blond hair was the single piece of gold that still glowed in the evening darkness of King David's estates. It was only after he disappeared with his sheep that the first evening star showed itself in the Eden sky.

We, that is, my friend Pisherl and I, lay down in the green grass. The strangeness of evening in an unfamiliar place frightened me a bit. But I recalled Laibl's blue eyes and his golden hair, and things seemed familiar to me again.

"We won't sleep tonight," Pisherl said. "Tonight, the angel Laibl will show us around King David's estates."

"More ghosts," I shivered. "Pisherl, why?"

"If a dummy asks 'why,' the answer is 'because.' "

The Eden sky had filled with stars. They flickered as if a wind were rocking them. It seemed to me I could hear the lullaby the wind was singing to the stars.

"Pisherl, do you hear?"

Pisherl lay with his eyes closed. He kept still.

VII

Night in King David's Estates

℘HE SHEPHERD ANGEL Laibl returned. The moon went up among the trees. Laibl put a finger to his mouth, "Psst . . . Let's go on tiptoe so that, God forbid, no one finds out that there are strangers abroad in King David's estates."

We got up from the grass and went after Laibl. We moved along byways, avoiding the main road. Laibl said it would be better that way. On the main road, God forbid, we might be met by one of King David's mistresses or a eunuch who would turn us both into pages.

At the thought of the word *page,* I shuddered. Pisherl reassured me. "Don't be frightened, Shmuel-Aba. Just let a eunuch try to get near us. We'll scratch his eyes out."

Laibl smiled. "Don't be such a tough guy, Pisherl. If there were only one eunuch in Eden, it would be all right, but there are a great many."

We went farther. At the slightest sound, we stopped, frightened lest we had been overheard. There were times when it seemed to us that we were being chased; that at any moment there would appear out of the bushes the plump shape of a eunuch who would laugh at the top of his voice—a greasy laughter, like olive oil. "I've caught you fellows," he'd say. "Now you'll be pages whether y' like it or not. 'N I'll get me 'nother gold star of David." But all our fears were for nothing. Laibl went before us; we followed. The Eden moon guarded us.

We heard the yearning call of an Eden cuckoo and the sweet trill of an Eden nightingale. "The cuckoo is having a conversation with the nightingale," Laibl said. "Every evening, the same conversation. I don't understand why they aren't bored."

"You can understand what they say, Laibl? Tell me, what do they say?" Pisherl asked.

"Of course I understand them," the angel Laibl said. "The cuckoo says, 'Cuck, cuck, how lovely are King David's estates.' And the nightingale answers, 'Really lovely. Oh my, oh my, how nice.' "

"Tell me, Laibl," I said to my new friend. "Why does King David go around with his crown forever on his head. He didn't take it off even when he was kissing Shulamith under the Eden oak."

"He wears his crown not only by day, but at night, also. He sleeps with it on his head. He's afraid . . ."

"What's he afraid of, Laibl?"

"Of King Saul, who is thrashing about to this day. He goes around complaining that King David took the crown from him. Soon, you'll see and hear what goes on in King David's estates at night. You'll hear King Saul's accusations and King David's reply."

"What answer does he give? Come on, Laibl. Tell me."

"You want to know? Oh brother, the answer he gives— that King David of ours. To every accusation, he replies by saying that Saul should take him to court."

We went farther. Almost, almost, I stepped on a ladybug. It was lucky for me that the angel Laibl pulled me back. The ladybug said a prayer of thanks for an escape from death and ran off quickly to disappear behind a mound of earth.

Before a densely branched, wide-spreading apple tree, the angel Laibl stopped. We, that is, my friend Pisherl and I, also stopped. Laibl whispered, "You see it, fellows. This is the Tree of Knowledge. This is the tree from which Eve plucked the apple; and that fool Adam was persuaded to taste it. You know the story; it's written in the Bible."

We stood and stared. It seemed to me that the Tree of Knowledge was a tree like any other in Eden; nevertheless, there was something different about it. Because of this tree, Adam and Eve had been driven from Eden. A wind sounded in the branches, but though the apples trembled, not one of them fell.

The moon that had been following us all this while cast its silver glow over the tree. It was something wonderful to behold. The angel Laibl whispered, "Let's hide nearby. You'll see something nice."

"What, for instance?" we asked, but he did not reply. He pointed at a bush, and we hid ourselves behind it. We lay still and waited. I don't recall how long we lay there. It might have been an hour, perhaps less. The angel Laibl suddenly pricked up his ears. We heard footsteps.

"Psst . . ." Laibl put a finger to his lips. "Psst . . . they're coming."

"Who? Who, Laibl?"

"Adam and Eve."

We saw two figures approaching the Tree of Knowledge. One of them was dressed in a frock coat and a top hat. The other wore hoopskirts and a hat with a long ostrich feather.

"That's it—that one," said the man with the top hat,

pointing. "That's the one, Eve. Right here, on this spot, you gave me the cursed apple to taste."

The woman in the hoopskirts sighed. She folded her hands over her heart. I could see tears in her eyes. *"Ah oui. This is it, Adam. It was the cursed serpent that persuaded me to it."*

"And *à cause de toi,* we've lost our happiness, Eve. That incomparable Paradise."

"It was a good life in Paradise, Adam, but that . . . that cursed . . ."

"Right . . . right, Eve," Adam replied, his finger pointing at his wife. "She, that cursed . . ."

"I meant the serpent, Adam. But you're pointing your finger at me."

"I too mean the serpent, Eve. And . . . I point my finger at you."

They began to quarrel. Each called the other every name under the sun. Eve grabbed a handful of Adam's hair. She herself might not have escaped unscathed, except that a miracle took place. An apple fell from the Tree of Knowledge, bounced off Adam's top hat, and fell to the grass.

"Don't touch it, Eve," Adam cried in a strange voice. "Don't touch it, I implore you, in God's name."

"God forbid," Eve said, clasping her hands together. "I can still taste that other apple."

They seated themselves under the tree. Adam reminded her of the fine times in Eden before their great sin. Eve's eyes glistened. "Ah, Adam. How good it was. We'll never see such times again."

"We were naked, unashamed, and happy," sighed Adam.

"Let's take off our clothes, Adam, and be naked, unashamed, and happy again."

"That's the one, Eve," said the man in the top hat

They got up and started to tear off their clothes. The stars twinkled wickedly in the sky. "Adam, I can't. The clothes have grown fast to my body," Eve sighed.

"Mine too." Adam bowed his head. They stood awhile with their heads bent, two lost figures in the light of the Eden moon. "Let's beg pardon for our sins. Let's beat our breasts," said Adam haltingly. "Maybe 'He' will forgive us."

They stood, facing the stars. The man in the top hat and the woman in the hoopskirts began to beat their breasts with their fists, whispering piously, imploring their Maker to forgive them, and to be shown the way back into Eden.

The wind, that all this while had been tickling the leaves on the Tree of Knowledge, suddenly leaped down. Adam and Eve were frightened; they took to their heels as fast as they could go.

Eve forgot her handbag in her flight. We opened it and found a mirror, a box of powder, and a love letter signed, "Your loving Max."

"Did you see that, fellows?" Laibl said. "Did you see how they said prayers for their sins? Every night they come to this place, where they sinned once. They steal into Eden and climb over the fence, so no one will notice them; then, at the slightest sound, they scamper off like Eden hares."

"But how do they get in? There are angels guarding the gates of Eden, night and day."

"Well, an angel is no more than an angel," explained Laibl. "Moreover, the watch is changed so rarely . . . not more than once every three years. No sooner does this exiled couple see that an angel is catching a nap, than they climb over the fence."

"Is it really true that they'll never be forgiven?" I asked.

"For the time being, they won't. It's said that when the

Messiah comes, there'll be a great amnesty. Meanwhile, these two hang around the gates of Eden."

I closed my eyes and imagined the luckless couple hovering about the gates. Angels stood there, carrying crooked scimitars in their hands. They waved their weapons, frightening anyone who approached Eden, the kingdom of the Zaddikim, without a permit.

"They deserve God's own pity," I said. "If I were the Messiah, I would come this very moment and open the gates of Eden."

"If . . ." Pisherl grumbled, "if grandma had wheels, she'd be a wagon."

I was annoyed that Pisherl was making fun of me, but I was so fond of him that I forgave him.

All this while, the angel Laibl was sitting, his head in his hands. Evidently, he was thinking. In the light of the moon, he looked exceedingly handsome. We looked with awe at this boy who looked after the sheep in King David's estates. We waited for him to rouse himself from his thoughts. Meanwhile, I watched the play of shadows thrown by the Tree of Knowledge. The shadows were continually nearing the circle of light that the moon cast around us, endeavoring to cross the boundary and withdrawing in fear. One bold shadow leaped into the circle and disappeared instantly, gone forever.

We heard the sound of trumpets. Laibl jumped up. "Come on, fellows. The trumpeter is calling all the pretty girls in King David's estates . . . all the forest maidens that live in the woods, all the water nymphs that live in the rivers. They're going to gather before King David's palace. He—King David, will sit on his balcony. He'll play on his harp, and they'll all dance the 'Good night, King David' dance."

We got up. Laibl went before us; we followed. Suddenly, the angel Laibl stopped. "Where is the moon?"

The moon had been following us, but now it had disappeared somewhere. We turned back and found it hanging, hooked in a thorn bush. The angel Laibl freed it, pricking his finger in the process. The moon shone once more over our heads, and we went on.

We stopped a hundred paces from King David's palace. We could see the king sitting on his balcony, his crown glittering on his head. On his right sat Bathsheba, a corpulent woman in a wig. She kept up a continual hiccuping. On his left sat Abishag, pale, and darkly dreamy-eyed. Her braids were coiled over her bosom like serpents.

King David was playing on his harp. The forest maidens, dressed in green gowns made of leaves, moved in a circle and sang:

> We are the maidens of the wood
> Who dance before you, King.
> We come from having put to sleep
> The woodbirds in their nests,
> The rabbits in their grasses,
> The butterflies in roses;
> Now we mean to rock to sleep
> The king David, our great lord,
> And his household too.
> Hear us. In our fluttering dance
> There sings the wind.

The dance of the forest maidens became livelier, quicker. King David smiled gently and a bit wearily. Abishag's eyes widened. Bathsheba swallowed her tenth yawn.

The forest maidens disappeared. The water nymphs in blue, gauzy gowns moved to the foreground. Water roses trembled in their hair. They sang:

> We, the nymphs who dwell in rivers,
> Dance before you now, King David;

> We have rocked and put to sleep
> The aged water mothers;
> But the lullaby that's fairest
> Is the murmuring of the waters.
> Now we mean to rock to sleep
> The king David, our great lord,
> And his household too.
> Hear us. In our fluttering dance
> There sings the wind.

The dance of the water nymphs could be heard rustling under the sound of the king's harp. Abishag's eyes became even more star-struck. Bathsheba wiped a dream from her left eye with a silk handkerchief.

Now the pretty daughters of the poor angels came to the foreground. They bowed before the king and sang:

> We, the maidens of the huts,
> All of us betrothed,
> Dance before you, David, king,
> You who live in happiness,
> Whom sorrows do not sting.

> We whom storms may buffet,
> On whom soft winds may blow
> Say good night, King David,
> And to your household, too.

The betrothed girls who lived in the clay huts danced, their rosy wings fluttering. With a shy "good night," they bowed and disappeared. King David rose and kissed Bathsheba's hand and Abishag's forehead. Then he went to his bedroom where he said a few chapters of the psalms and settled down to sleep. He left the harp on the balcony so that the wind might play it through the night.

His wives sat a while longer on the balcony and looked dreamily up at the stars, silently cursing each other. The first to get up was Bathsheba; she went off to her apartment without a word. Abishag continued to sit watching the stars; then, on tiptoe, she went into David's bedroom.

"Come, fellows," said the angel Laibl. "Let's go down to the river. We'll come back here around midnight. Then you'll see something lovely." We went to the river. We passed a number of poor huts. Through their open windows, we could hear the snoring of the exhausted angels. On a bench before one of the huts, there sat two young female angels. One of them had a letter in her hand.

"Read it. Read your letter for me, Pessl. I want to hear what your Froim writes," pleaded one of the angels.

Pessl opened the letter and began to read by the light of the stars. We could hear the trembling of her voice. " 'My dear Pessl,' " she read, " 'you should know that for the last three days, our regiment has been quartered on the boundary of the Turkish Eden. Military service here is very hard. We have to be continually on guard against Turkish tobacco smugglers. Our commander, the angel Captain Shimshun, has told us that, because whole sacks of Turkish tobacco are being smuggled into the Jewish Eden, there is less snuff being taken, and the Jewish snuff monopoly is suffering extremely. Any of us who catches a smuggler has the right to break his wings. We are on the alert, night and day, but as yet we've caught nobody. It would seem that the smugglers know that the Seventh Angelic Regiment of the Jewish Eden isn't going to tolerate any monkey business, and they're watching out for their wings. How long we're to be stationed at the border, I don't know. I know only that I can hardly wait for the day when I get my discharge . . . in one year and two months. We'll be married just as soon as I get home. Until that happy time comes, I send you love and kisses . . . love and kisses. Your Froim.' "

When she had finished reading the letter, the angel Pessl

folded it and put it in her bosom. "May my prayers protect him," she said.

The other angel kept silent. I could tell that she was envious of her friend. An angel . . . a soldier . . . a hero . . . If only God would grant her such luck.

I tugged at Pisherl's right wing. "Some letter, Pisherl. That Froim knows how to write a letter. What do you say, Pisherl?"

Pisherl did not answer. The angel Laibl gave a soft whistle. "Come on, fellows, let's go."

We went toward the river. I kept looking back. The two girlfriends continued to sit on the bench, one with a letter, the other without a letter. The longing of one had an address: "Infantry Soldier, the Angel Froim, at the Border of the Turkish Eden." The longing of the other searched for an address.

"Perhaps we shouldn't have listened," I said. "I'm afraid we may have committed a great sin."

"What . . . huh . . . d'you say something, Shmuel-Aba? What did you say?" Pisherl started up, as if from sleep.

"I didn't say anything, Pisherl. You're just imagining things." Suddenly I felt that it would be a sin to talk of sin at such a moment.

We went on. The shepherd angel Laibl went first; we followed.

"Shmuel-Aba."

"What? You called me, Pisherl?"

"Me. You're dreaming, Shmuel-Aba."

"Maybe it was you, Laibl. Was it you who called me by name?"

"Are you talking in your sleep, Shmuel-Aba?" Laibl looked at me, puzzled.

I thought, "But something just went by and called me by name. I clearly heard someone." But then I concluded,

"Maybe I did imagine it. That must be it; I imagined it."
I didn't know at that time that there is a silence in Eden
that can call you by name so clearly that it can be heard.

We heard the sound of the river and began to walk
faster. The sound was closer.

The great clock that hung in King David's palace began
to sound. I counted, "One, two, three, four . . ."

"Ten. Ten o'clock," my friend Pisherl said.

"We can spend about two hours at the river," the shepherd angel Laibl observed. "We have to be back at the
palace at twelve. That's when it begins."

"What?" Pisherl and I asked.

Laibl smiled. "You'll see for yourselves." But his smile
disappeared in a second. We approached the river; it
curled like a silver ribbon, dazzling our eyes.

We sat down at its edge. None of us said a word; only
the river murmured. I put my feet into the water. It was
cool and gentle.

My friend Pisherl tossed a pebble into the water. "What
have you done?" Laibl asked, grabbing him by the arm.
But it was too late. The pebble Pisherl had thrown into
the river woke the water nymph Sarah-Gitl. She rose up
from the depths, her hair a tangle, her eyes filled with
sleep.

"Who threw the stone? Who woke me up?"

"I," said Pisherl, "but I didn't mean to do it."

The water nymph was an old maid who suffered from
sleeplessness. She always took a sleeping pill before going
to bed. "Because you've wakened me," she said to Pisherl,
"you'll have to be my bridegroom."

Pisherl turned white as chalk. His teeth chattered. Luckily for him, Laibl took a hand in the matter. "What do you
need a bridegroom for?" he said to the water nymph.

"You've gotten along all these years without one; you can get along without one from now on."

The water nymph began to yell, "How am I going to get back to sleep? I've taken my last sleeping pill and the pharmacy is closed. How am I going to get back to sleep?"

"You're talking nonsense, Sarah-Gitl. You don't need a bridegroom to put you to sleep. I'll fix it so you can fall asleep again." With that, Laibl began to meow like a cat. He gave us the signal to do the same thing. We made such cat's music that the water nymph turned green and yellow. She clutched her head with both hands and shrieked aloud. But we didn't quit until she dived into the water after heaping deadly curses on us. "Now," said the angel Laibl, "let's beat it."

We spread our wings and took off, like the arrow from its bow. "You've saved my life," Pisherl said to Laibl. "Before I'd be the bridegroom of that monster of ugliness, I'd be a page in King David's palace."

I asked, "How did you know that the water nymph could not abide the meowing of cats, Laibl?"

"It's a fine story, and a short one," said Laibl. "The water nymph had a bridegroom once . . . pfoo . . . what am I saying? There was talk of a betrothal. The prospective groom came to see her, and to be seen by her. A cat got mixed up in it and the marriage never took place."

"What do you mean, 'A cat got mixed up in it and the marriage never took place'?"

"While they—the couple, that is—were sitting in the house talking, the cat spilled a pot of sour cream; the bridegroom's clothes were spattered and he went away angry, calling the nymph a slob, saying he never wanted to hear, or even think, of her again. Ever since then, she's been an old maid. She suffers from sleeplessness; and no sooner does she hear the meowing of a cat, than she's ready to leap into the fire."

My friend Pisherl said the blessing for an escape from danger, but he continued to be fearful for a considerable while just the same. He calmed down only when we were out of earshot of the river. Then he spat three times: "To her head; to her hands and feet; to her body and soul." We burst into giggles; Laibl laughed so hard that he could hardly catch his breath.

"This time, Pisherl, you got away with a scare. Be careful of a second time."

Once again, we alighted. It was still some time till twelve, and we had no need to hurry. We sat at the edge of a plowed field and the angel Laibl piped softly. Pisherl was thinking, and I was busy counting the stars.

I have loved counting stars for as long as I can remember. I've never counted them in order to know how many there are. It's the counting itself that's important. I never tire of starting the count all over again.

How long we sat at the edge of the field, I can't tell you for certain. Laibl's voice cut across my counting and Pisherl's thinking. "Fellows, come on. It's time to go."

We went a short distance on foot and flew the rest of the way, arriving at King David's palace seven minutes before twelve. We hid among the trees, where we lay down and waited.

The seven minutes dragged like an eternity.

VIII

Midnight in King David's Estates

Ｔ HE MOON CLOCK on King David's tower struck twelve.
We lay under the trees holding our breath. What was it
that was about to happen at this midnight hour in King
David's estates? "It's the hour for ghosts," I thought, but I
could not bring myself to say a word.

The moon above our heads was growing larger, more
imposing; the stars more distant and fearsome. I could
hear the beating of my friend Pisherl's heart.

There was a harp on King David's balcony. The wind
kept trying to play it without success. I thought, "It's a
cripple, God help us. The king is more skillful than that.
A pity he's asleep while the dilletantish wind keeps up its
silly tinkling. It's enough to hurt one's ears."

Suddenly, it was quiet. The wind hid itself somewhere.
Bathsheba, wearing only her nightgown, appeared on the
balcony. Her eyes were red with weeping, and it was evi-
dent that she had not yet slept at all. For a while she
listened to the silence, and when she saw that everyone in
the palace was asleep, she went down the marble stairs.

Barefooted and dressed only in her nightgown, she stood

in the empty square before the palace. I watched her closely. She was old and ugly; her face was wrinkled. Even the indiscriminate wind was not tempted to play with her nightgown. "A real hag," I said softly.

"Once she was young and beautiful," the angel Laibl said. "Now she is old—and that's why she knows the holy books by heart."

"Ah, now I understand." Pisherl exclaimed. "She got up to say her midnight prayers."

"This time, you're absolutely wrong," Laibl said. "She is, indeed, pious, but a woman is always a woman. No sooner does she sense that Abishag is with the king, than she's unable to sleep. She loves the king dearly and it follows, therefore, that she hates Abishag. She could wish her drowned in a teaspoon of water."

"Ah! Now I understand," I said, and still did not understand why Bathsheba had risen at the time for midnight prayers and was standing in her nightgown in the open square before the palace.

"Does this help her any?" I asked Laibl, the shepherd angel.

"It looks as if she's arranged a meeting with the sorceress. When poor Bathsheba sees that Abishag's beauty is more powerful than her prayers, she calls in the sorceress to give her remedies that will win her the heart of her beloved king."

"Do the remedies help?" Pisherl asked without taking his eyes from the fat woman in the nightgown.

"The way leeches help the dead," Laibl whispered. "But she won't let up. She continues to believe that the sorceress will find herbs that will help her."

Bathsheba stood frozen, moving not so much as an eye. All at once, she shuddered. We could hear her whispering

. . . calling. "Genendl. Genendl. Where are you, damn it?"

"Majesty, I am here."

We saw an old woman wrapped in a Turkish shawl. She was lame on one foot. Limping, she approached Bathsheba.

"I almost froze to death, Genendl. Where were you?"

The old sorceress did not reply. She took Bathsheba by the hand and led her to a garden bench that stood near the palace. Bathsheba sat on the bench; the old woman sat at her feet.

"You have problems, my daughter?" the old woman said, and a rotten tooth, the sole inhabitant of her mouth, reflected the moon's bright light for a moment.

"Ah—God in heaven," Bathsheba sighed. "Advise me, Auntie. I can't stand it any longer. My heart will break."

"The girl is with him again, Bathsheba?"

"Yes," sighed Bathsheba. "No sooner does he go to sleep, than she steals into his room on tiptoe. God grant she may fall and break her neck. God in heaven!"

"And you've spoken to him," the sorceress murmured, "and told him what I taught you to say?"

"Dearest Genendl, I wept before him. I told him that on his account, my Uriah, who never treated me ill, who gave me my heart's desire—may he be blessed with a happy Eden—was taken from the world. He never called me anything but sweetheart. 'And I gave all that up—for you, David,' I said. 'And this is how you repay me in my old age?' "

"Well," the sorceress inquired. "What did he say?"

"What did he say? You really want to know? Better not ask, Genendl. He patted my wig and said, 'Dear Bathsheba. If you were still as lovely and young as you were then, I would see my way to getting rid of your husband once again. But now, as you are . . . God bless you . . . in your old age, I would spend a fortune to bring him back to life. I would lead you both under the wedding canopy and give you my blessing.' "

Bathsheba began to cry. The old sorceress comforted her, patted her hands, and spoke consolingly, "Don't cry, Bathsheba. It'll be all right, despite Abishag."

The old woman took out a pack of cards. She spread them out on the ground and studied them a long, long time.

"She's reading cards. D'you see, Pisherl?" I called to my friend.

"In the light of the moon, Bathsheba looks better than she did before," Pisherl said, as if to himself.

"It's not the first or the last time Genendl's been here. She comes every Thursday and reads the cards under the stars."

"And Bathsheba believes in it?" I asked.

"She believes. And for a while, her belief turns her lovely. It's a pity King David doesn't see her now. She would certainly please him," the angel Laibl said.

The sorceress rose and danced several times around her cards that lay spread out on the ground. Bathsheba sat as if carved in stone. The sorceress lifted her head to the stars. Her gray hair was disordered. She spread her hands and made an incantation, "From the hills of Eden, come, my sparrow hawks. All seven of you, come. Aunt Genendl calls you . . . Aunt Genendl implores you. Obey the call, my hawks. Shake the sleep from your wings. Your Aunt Genendl needs your advice. Your Aunt Genendl has a prayer. You, who peck at the stars with your beaks. Come flying. One . . . two . . . I'll count thirteen."

She repeated the incantation several times. Then she sat

down on the ground and waited, curling herself up into a ball.

"Pisherl, I'm scared." I huddled up against my friend who lay near me.

"Psst," the angel Laibl put a finger to his lips. "Hush up."

We heard the fluttering of wings. The seven hawks of the Eden mountains were circling in the air. Then, they settled at Genendl the sorceress' feet. "I have called you, oh hawks . . ." The old woman caressed the wings of her hawks one by one. "I have called on you at this midnight hour, oh faithful ones, so that you may help me . . . so that you may bring me a sovereign remedy that will help the bruised soul of Bathsheba (may she live long), who is sitting here on the garden bench and can find no rest on account of the great love she bears for King David—long life to him."

"Command us, Auntie Genendl," the chief of the hawks said. "Command us and we'll bring you anything that is in our power to bring. But there is one condition, Auntie Genendl. You must finish telling us the story you started six hundred thousand years ago."

"Good," the sorceress said. "Agreed. I'll finish the story after you've flown off and brought me the love-me flower from the Eden mountains, and the yearn-for-me flower, and the die-for-me rose from the rivers of Eden."

"Good, Auntie Genendl," the chief of the hawks said. "We'll fly away and do our best to bring you what you need. But remember that when—God willing—we bring you what you want, you keep your word."

"If Auntie Genendl promises, it's promised," the sorceress snapped. "Don't lose any time, my hawks. Fly, search, and bring what I commanded. When do you expect you'll be back?"

"When do we expect . . ." The chief hawk considered a moment. "That's something we can't say for sure. But I can promise you it'll be on a Thursday night. Let's hope it won't be too long."

The hawks spread their wings and flew away. Genendl the sorceress looked after them and smiled. "They're loyal fellows—those Eden hawks. No sooner called for, they come, ready to answer any request. Fly in good health, my hawks, and come back bringing Bathsheba the good fortune she dreams of."

Bathsheba still sat like a statue. Her eyes mirrored the stars.

"Go, dear Bathsheba. Go, daughter. Go. Go on to bed," the old sorceress said, caressing her wig. "Go. You'll only catch cold, God forbid, with only your nightgown on. It'll be all right, daughter. On a Thursday . . . you heard them . . . my hawks will bring the flowers. You'll brew a tea with them, and you'll give it to King David to drink. It'll be all right, Bathsheba. It'll be all right, my daughter."

Bathsheba rose from the garden bench. She started up the marble steps like a sleepwalker. Suddenly she stopped. Turning her head toward the sorceress who stood below, she said, "If only they aren't deceiving you, Genendl. I couldn't endure it, Genendl. I would go mad."

"What are you talking about, my daughter?" The sorceress spat three times. "May your enemies go mad. My darling, God willing . . . you'll find happiness yet."

We watched as the old sorceress limped away and disappeared into the forest. Bathsheba continued to stand on the staircase, hesitating. A beam of moonlight searched for lice in her wig.

For a while, she stood still. Who knows what was going on in her heart? Then she shuddered and started up the stairs again. The window of King David's bedroom was open. Bathsheba listened beside it, but she was afraid to look in. She would have burst with envy.

"If only the hawks do not deceive me," she murmured. "No. Auntie Genendl's hawks are not deceitful," she consoled herself. Then she went to her bedroom.

I poked my friend. "Pisherl. Did you see?"

"Why not? Am I blind?"

"And you heard, Pisherl? You heard everything?"

"Why not? Of course I heard. What am I? Deaf?"

Once again, Laibl the shepherd angel put his finger to his mouth. "Psst. Fellow, psst. You can discuss it some other time."

We held our breath. Each of us wondered what was going to happen next, but we were too scared to say a word. We heard the gallop of a horse. "Who can it be?" I wondered, and yet I was afraid to ask. We saw a rider on a white horse. He was dressed in armor that glittered in the moonlight. The rider leaped from his horse, approached King David's palace, and called in a loud voice, "Hey, David. Get up. Let's fight."

No one stirred in the palace. Only the wind moved in the draperies of King David's bedroom. But the rider in the iron armor would not let up. He stretched an ironclad arm out and cried even louder, "Hey, David. Get up. Come on outside . . . in the open field . . . to fight."

King David came out on the balcony rubbing his sleep-laden eyes and swallowing a delicious yawn. He said to the rider who stood below, "Is it you, Saul? Why won't you let me sleep?"

King Saul burst into piercing, bitter laughter. "Come on down, David. Let's fight now. Come on outside and fight."

King David yawned again. "I don't want to fight with

you, Saul. I came to Eden to rest—to be happy—not to fight."

"Coward," King Saul thundered. "Coward. You're afraid to fight. Then give me back my crown, coward. Give the crown back at once, do you hear?"

"Don't get excited, Saul," King David said gently. "Why are you getting excited? You know it accomplishes nothing. Take my advice and get back on your horse. Go on back to the World of Errors. What good does it do you, to keep the Zaddikim from their rest?"

King David's gentle manner exasperated the armored rider beyond measure. He shouted so loudly, he woke the birds in their nests. "Just look at him. The Zaddik in furs. The thief stole King Saul's crown, and yet he calls himself a Zaddik. Steeped in sin from top to toe, and yet he calls himself a Zaddik."

Apparently, King David was used to such nighttime visits. He stood calmly on his balcony and tried to placate the enraged horseman. But nothing would do. King Saul became ever more angry. His eyes all but blazed. "Give me back my crown. Do you hear? The crown. Give it back. I won't stir from this spot until you give it back."

Saul's shouts wakened Abishag. Frightened, she ran to the window and asked King David, "What's happening, David dear? Who's shouting so?" David reassured her. He kissed her forehead and told her to go back to sleep. He would follow shortly.

Abishag looked like a frightened doe. Her whole body trembled as she said pleadingly, "I'm going, David, but see that you don't wait too long. I beg you." She crept off to bed. King Saul continued to stand below, shaking his fists at David, threatening, accusing, demanding the crown back, as well as the throne of Eden, which, according to him, David had stolen too.

We saw a rider on a white horse

Finally, King David could control himself no longer. Raising his nightgown, he said loudly, "Kiss my . . ."

"Thief," cried the armor-clad rider. "You stole the crown from me, and the 'Kiss my' verse from your son Solomon."

King David went back to his bedroom, closed the door that looked out on the balcony, and drew the curtains over the window.

King Saul mounted his horse, and galloped several times around the palace. His fist raised to the stars, he cried, "I'll be revenged. Don't think for a moment that we're finished. I'll be revenged. May God almighty be my help."

I clung to my friend Pisherl. He, in turn, crept closer to Laibl, the shepherd angel. "Did you see that, friends?" Laibl whispered. "He always rides up like this, that fellow from the World of Errors, and wakes King David. It's the same old story, every time he comes. The same old conversation, word for word. He doesn't omit so much as a syllable of his complaints. Until at last, King David lifts his nightgown and says, 'Kiss my . . .'"

"And now he's ridden off in anger, his face all contorted. Where do you suppose he's going?" I asked.

"Let's follow him," suggested the angel Laibl. "But be quiet—don't make a sound. He mustn't notice he's being followed or observed."

We spread our wings and flew, quietly flapping our wings. We hardly breathed.

King Saul was riding his white horse. His tall, lean shape made a disturbing outline against the moonlit sky. Laibl whispered, "A restless soul. He had no rest on Earth, and he has no rest in this world. His restlessness is devouring him now that he's dead as much as it did when he was alive."

Before a small, whitewashed house, King Saul stopped

his horse. He leaped down, and with jangling spurs, approached the window.

"The prophet Samuel lives here," explained Laibl. "He's still a bachelor . . . that is, he's unwed. He lives modestly; doesn't mix in the politics of Eden. Sossl, a female angel with warts, serves him. She does his bit of cooking and patches his shirts. The old fellow doesn't need anything more. He's promised me that when the Messiah comes, he'll let me have his share of the Messiah-Ox and of the Leviathan. All he wants set aside for himself is a little bit of the Messiah wine."

King Saul knocked at the window. Once, twice, three times. Each time he knocked more loudly than before, crying out, "Samuel. Samuel . . . prophet. Get up. It's me."

The door opened. The old prophet Samuel came out. His beard was snow-white, his eyes were weak with age and he was slightly deaf. "Are you here again?" asked the prophet Samuel. "Why won't you let me sleep?" King Saul's imposing figure seemed to shrink. He bowed before the old prophet. "Help me find my father's mules. How can I go back without my father's mules? I . . . a herdsman."

The old prophet smiled bitterly. His white beard trembled like a distress signal in wind at night. "You'll never find the mules again, Saul. That's over and done with. You'll never be a herdsman again. Someone else has the flock."

"Neither herdsman nor king," Saul sobbed. "What then, prophet? What then? Tell me. Advise me."

The old prophet waved a hand, then shook his white beard. The stars above the quiet house grew larger, more sorrowful. "You want to know 'What then,' Saul? How should I know? I was a prophet on Earth. Here, in the Real World, I live off the pension that was set aside for me because of my good deeds. How should I know, Saul? How should I know?"

The armor-clad rider bowed his head. His whole body emanated grief. It made me desperately sad. King Saul mounted his horse, pulled on the reins and said, "Up, Eagle. Up. Back to the World of Errors." The horse flew off like the wind. All we could see were the sparks that spurted from his horseshoes. Old Samuel the prophet looked after the grieving rider until he had disappeared. The old man sighed and went back into the house on tiptoe, in order not to wake his cook.

We all sat down at the side of the road. Each of us was lost in thought. The stars over our heads turned pale. A cool wind took its first promenade over King David's estates.

Two shadows fell across the road. Raising our eyes, we saw two peasant angels in flight. They were flying so low, we could hear every word they said.

"If only they don't catch us, Zainvl," one angel said. "We'd be in a real fix then. First we'd be beaten, and then—the shame and the pain."

"Let's not even think of it, Elimelekh," the second one said. "And let's hope we'll make it. Life in King David's estates is no longer bearable. One toils all day long, and never has enough to eat. No sooner do you complain a bit than you're beaten. We're treated like animals, not like angels."

"You're right. Of course. But when I remember the children . . . my heart breaks . . . poor things. How are they guilty?"

"That's the way it is with me," the second one sighed. "But never mind. Let's try our luck abroad. It's become unendurable here."

The two angels disappeared. We looked after them with

pity. I prayed that the escape would succeed and that they might find work abroad.

Evidently, Laibl understood what I was whispering to myself. He looked at me for a while, then said, "Fools. Where are they running? Are things better anywhere else? Let's assume the escape is successful. For that sort of angel, Eden is not Eden."

Laibl's words cast a pall over my spirits. I pitied the escaping angels as well as those who remained behind. I imagined their wives when they woke up the next morning. I could hear the weeping of the two miserable, abandoned women and the wailing of the children.

The door of the prophet Samuel's house opened. The old man came out again. Evidently, after King Saul's visit, he had been unable to fall asleep. He paced back and forth before his house, back and forth, apparently waiting for the day to dawn.

"What are we sitting here for?" Laibl asked. "Let's fly back to King David's palace." We flew back. One by one, the stars began to go out. It turned cool in Eden.

We settled down before the palace. It was quiet on all sides. There was not the slightest sound to be heard.

Somewhere, a rooster crowed. A second one replied. Then there was such a crowing that I thought I would be deafened. The chief of the Eden roosters appeared on King David's tower—a fellow with a coral comb. He set up such a crowing, such a flapping of wings that he extinguished the moon.

The clay huts began to stir. The angels woke from their sleep and began getting ready to go to work.

Laibl told us he had to get his flock out to pasture. Meanwhile, we were to fly on ahead and wait for him till he got back with his sheep. He showed us where to wait. As it turned out, it was the very same hill where we had first met him.

"Get going, fellows, or, God forbid, someone'll spot you."

He went off to the stables and we, Pisherl and I, spread our wings. We flew off in the direction Laibl had shown us. On the little green hill, we settled down. The grass was wet. We were tired from our wakeful night. The blue dawn had begun to spread over King David's estates. The birds twittered and greeted each other, taking pleasure in the new day in Eden.

"Pisherl, what do you think of our night in King David's estates?"

"What should I think, Shmuel-Aba? It was some night! We'll have things to tell our children and our grandchildren."

In the distance we could hear the peasant angels singing as they went to work. The song grew louder, then softer, and finally it ended entirely.

"Where do you suppose Laibl is, Pisherl?" I asked.

"How should I know, Shmuel-Aba. He'll be here soon, no doubt. After all, he knows we're waiting for him."

It was not long before Laibl showed up. He was driving the flock before him, playing on his pipe. He sat down near us. From his pack, he took black bread and a hunk of sheep's cheese. We ate and said farewell to our friend.

"Come again," Laibl said. "I'll treat you like honored guests. See that you don't wait too long." We kissed each other good-by. It seemed a pity to leave such a handsome, barefoot angel, but we had to. No doubt Pisherl's mother was worried about her son.

Near my home, I said good-by to my dear friend. We agreed that we would tell no one where we had been or what we had seen. We took our solemn oath on it, then we flew off in different directions, Pisherl to his home, and I to mine.

I stopped my narrative. Dawn was already at the window. Opposite me, the rabbi sat. His white beard trembled; his eyes were red with astonishment and lack of sleep. "Wonder of wonders," he said. "A great lord, our King David. Some fortune . . . God be praised. May he use it in good health."

The rabbinical judge sat with his mouth open so wide, one could count his teeth. He said not a word.

Only the rich man, Reb Mikhel Hurvitz, drummed with his fingers on his belly and, unless I'm mistaken, said the German word *sonderbar* at least a hundred times.

My mother struck her hands together. "Ah . . . a mother's troubles . . . the dawn is here and the child hasn't closed an eye. Bandits . . . why are you picking on him?"

"I . . . I . . . What do you want of me, Zelda? Who's picking on the child?"

My mother did not answer him. She merely cast a look in his direction and my father began to tremble. If he hadn't been holding on to the table, who knows what might have happened?

My mother snatched me up in her arms. She almost choked me with her kisses.

"Come, my darling. Come to sleep. Woe to your mother . . ."

She put me in the cradle and began to rock it. I was tired and the rocking tired me even more. A moment before I fell asleep, I raised myself up and told the honored guests not to come that night because I was too weary. Tomorrow evening, God willing, I would go on with my narrative of Eden.

I lay back in my cradle. I could hear the door opening

with a creak, and the guests saying good-by to my father; then my eyes began to stick fast. I fell asleep.

In my dream, I relived the night in King David's estates. In it, I saw my friend Pisherl again, and heard Laibl, the angel shepherd boy, singing his songs. In that same dream, I recounted my remarkable experiences in Eden to the rabbi, the rabbinical judge, and to Reb Mikhel Hurvitz, the rich man.

IX

A Terrible Tale of the Messiah-Ox

I SLEPT through the entire day. Everyone went around on tiptoe in order not to wake me, God forbid. My father didn't dare to raise his head. To say so much as a word was out of the question, and he wandered about like a shadow. My mother took good care that my sleep should be undisturbed.

When I woke in the evening, the house was almost dark. My father was standing in a corner saying the *Shmone-Esre* prayer. I wiped my eyes, yawned deliciously and called my mother to the cradle-side. "Momma, will you let me nurse, please? I haven't had a thing to eat all day. You know very well that I don't eat anything when I'm asleep." My mother required no urging. She nursed me at once, caressing and kissing me all the while, as is the custom of mothers.

"They've been torturing you, my son. Whoever heard of such a thing—grown men, and they won't let an infant sleep. He has to tell them stories of Eden all night long. And it's all . . ." she turned to my father who was just finishing the *Schmone-Esre* prayer, "and it's all your fault,

123

shlimmazel. Are you a father? You're a Tartar, not a father."

My father turned pale. He was unprepared for this sort of treatment at the moment. He did not reply, but acted as if my mother meant someone else. I defended him, saying, "Leave Daddy alone, Momma. He's not to blame. I asked him myself to invite those people so that I could tell them how things are in Eden. Tomorrow night, God willing, they'll come again, and I'll go on with my story."

I fell asleep once more. I was so tired that I was not even able to wish my mother a good night. I don't remember clearly what I dreamed that night, and what I can't remember clearly, I don't want to talk about.

When I woke in the morning, the room was already filled with sunlight. My mother was not in the house. She had gone out to milk the goat. Our cat was warming itself on the window sill.

"Here, kitty, kitty," I called. It leaped down from the window and crept into the cradle with me. It licked my eyelids clean; I felt as if I were newly born.

The day passed without any remarkable happenings. We ate breakfast. After lunch, my father took a little nap, and my mother gossiped with the women outdoors. I played with a red quilt-button.

As was his custom, my father went to the synagogue in the evening. This evening, he did not stay there very long but returned home soon.

We ate supper . . . rice with milk. It was not much later that the rabbi, the rabbinical judge, and the rich man came in with a "good evening."

They sat down at the table. The rabbi was even paler than he had been the night before; the rabbinical judge was even more withered. Only the rich man, Mikhel Hurvitz, looked the same. His gold sparkled. To everything that was said, he nodded his head and said in German, *"Sonderbar."*

I sat down opposite the rabbi. The lamp burned on the table and my mother had darkened the windows. Everyone was ready to listen. My mother stood, as usual, near the door, her hands folded over her heart. She said, "Don't tire yourself out, my treasure. If you get tired, rest awhile. It isn't as if there were a fire, God forbid. Nothing for you to hurry about. If you get hungry, tell me at once and I'll nurse you." My mother, blessings on her head, was being careful of me. She protected me like the apple of her eye.

Resting my head in my hands, I resumed my narrative. Everyone around the table sat hushed and silent. Every heartbeat could be heard.

As you know, I said, I bade my friend Pisherl good-by. He flew off to his home, and I to mine. I was so tired, I could hardly keep erect; my wings were soiled. It was all I could do to drag myself home.

I collapsed on my bed and slept. In my dream, King David, Bathsheba, Abishag, water nymphs, King Saul, and the sorceress Genendl were mixed up in a topsy-turvy sequence. People and things were so tangled that the dream became even more nightmarish than the reality had been.

I woke around four o'clock in the afternoon. I washed, snatched a bite to eat and was off, flying to my friend Pisherl's.

He was still asleep, and I sat down in the workroom to wait until he woke up.

Pisherl's father, Shlomo-Zalman the patch-tailor, was standing at the big table with his tape measure around his neck and a piece of chalk in his hand. He was marking a pair of wings that had been given him for repair.

The two apprentice angels Berl and Siomkeh sat at the

Shlomo-Zalman the patch-tailor was standing
at the large table

worktable engrossed in their work. Their needles practically flew in their fingers. I tried to count how many stitches each of them made in a minute but was unable to. I kept miscounting.

Pisherl's mother, the angel Hannah-Deborah, came in from the alcove. She sat down beside me and tried to find out where we . . . that is, Pisherl and I . . . had gotten lost. She had thought that we were in who-knows-what sort of trouble, and had wanted to call the Eden police, or to raise a fuss so we might be searched for.

I didn't know whether I ought to tell her the truth. I had forgotten completely to come to an understanding with my friend Pisherl about this matter. For a while, I sat undecided, sighing. Yes? Or no? And I concluded finally that I was not obliged to tell her the truth. If Pisherl wanted to tell her, then it was up to him. I acted dumb and said that I hadn't seen Pisherl in some three days. In fact, I had only come to find out whether, God forbid, he might not be sick.

"Sick?" The angel Hannah-Deborah clasped her hands together. "May my enemies be sick. That's all I need, for Pisherl to be sick. Oh, a mother's griefs."

She went on trying to get something out of me, but when she saw that I wouldn't change my story—which was that I knew nothing about anything—she shook her head and went back to the alcove.

Pisherl's father finished marking the wings. Siomkeh too completed the pair he had been working on. They were now ready to be fitted, and Pisherl's father flew off with them to his customer, Henzl the miller. No sooner had he left the house, than the angel Siomkeh began to sing.

> A love affair's not worth the while,
> Angels, I implore you;

> Heed my words, send love away,
> It will be better for you.
>
> Ah, love is pain, and love is sorrow
> And paid for with a wealth of tears;
> By day, it keeps you from your labors,
> Your nights are sleepless with its cares.

Berl, the second apprentice angel, who was at sword's points with Siomkeh, was, in this case, in agreement with his enemy. He cleared his throat and sang loudly:

> See, how your luck is fair a while,
> With blossom, star, and bird;
> Then it runs off a thousand miles—
> It's enough to drive you mad.
>
> But madness isn't worth the while,
> Angels, I implore you;
> Wish love far off, deep underground,
> It will be better for you.

I was quite distressed by this song. I remembered the moonlit night when I had seen these two enamored apprentice angels bump into each other on the sidewalk. "They don't even know that I saw them and heard their conversation," I thought. Nevertheless, my heart continued to feel heavy.

In the alcove Pisherl's sister Ettl, the lovely angel with the rose-colored wings, began to sing. Evidently she did not agree with the moral of the songs sung by the two apprentice tailors. Her voice was as sweet as sugar; *her* song was lively and joyful:

> You came to me in a dream—
> My golden life, my dear.
> You gave me a ring of gold
> To be my souvenir.

The golden ring is lovely,
I wear it night and day;
I've shown it to my schoolmate
And told her what to say.

My bridegroom bought the ring;
He has a clear bright glance.
If I had permission,
I'd fly to him at once.

I would stay with him, always—
A hundred years or so;
Until my fine black tresses
Should turn as white as snow.

"Now who's supposed to know which of the songs is right," I thought. "Those fellows say one thing, then Pisherl's sister comes and says the contrary. When I grow up," I thought, "I'll know the difference clearly."

The angel Siomkeh sighed. He was remembering the Eden grocer's daughter, and his heart ached. I could see for myself how a tear fell from his eyes onto a wing he was repairing.

Berl was jealous of his colleague because of the tear. He thought long about the Eden grocer's daughter, squeezing his eyes as hard as he could, and succeeded at last in shedding a tear. He cast a triumphant glance at the angel Siomkeh. It was a speaking look: "What did you suppose? Did you think you were the only one who could sacrifice a tear for her?"

Evidently, Berl's tear distressed Siomkeh. He bowed his head and worked even faster with his needle as he sang.

Dear, because you mocked me
My grief is now complete;
You shamed me, and I wander
Nightly through the street.

> The moon brings greetings from you,
> And a thousand stars above
> And yet I cannot reach you;
> I am deceived by love.

The angel Berl pushed himself away from the work-table, irritated by Siomkeh's song. He felt that if Siomkeh were to sing another stanza, then he, Berl, would be unable to control himself any longer. He would catch up the iron and split his head. Luckily, Siomkeh ran out of thread and the song had only two stanzas. Berl calmed down.

Well, "calmed down" is one way of saying it. What turmoil might be going on in his heart, God alone knew. Outwardly, at least, he was calm.

Pisherl woke up. He was delighted when, on coming into the workroom, he discovered I was there. He ran up and embraced me as if we hadn't seen each other in years.

"Have you been here long, Shmuel-Aba?"

"I've been waiting for more than an hour. Praise God, you've had a good sleep."

We went over to the open window and looked out. There, in the meadow, the Messiah-Ox was grazing. The three barefooted angels who looked after him were playing cards.

I said to my friend, "The Messiah-Ox gets fatter every year. By the time the Messiah comes, he'll be too fat to move."

Pisherl was silent. We saw the angel Khasya walking across the Eden meadow. She was in her ninth month, and she took a walk every evening to get a bit of fresh air. "Pisherl, why is she wearing a red apron?" I asked my friend. "If the Messiah-Ox sees it, God forbid, there may be an accident."

"You're right. That's right," said Pisherl. And both of us began to signal to her, waving our hands, motioning to the pregnant angel to turn back, in God's name, while there was still time. But the angel Khasya didn't understand our signals. She went peacefully on, getting closer to the place where the Messiah-Ox was grazing. The Messiah-Ox saw the red apron and his eyes lighted up. We thought that at any moment he would fling himself at her.

But we were mistaken. He did not take kindly to the red apron, it is true, but to our great surprise, he kept his peace. Evidently, it occurred to him that he was no ordinary ox. He was, indeed, the Messiah-Ox, for whom it was not fitting to fly into a rage over a piece of red cloth, like a common bull. Nevertheless, it was fated that a calamity should happen.

The angel Khasya was by no means overly bright. One might say that there was more beast in her than in the Messiah-Ox. When she was quite close, only a few paces from the grazing animal, she stopped to watch his pleasant cud-chewing. She stood for a while, admiring his appetite. The three barefooted angels were quarreling over their cards. One argued this way, the other that way, and the third disagreed with the other two. They were so engrossed by their quarrel that they did not notice that the pregnant angel went up to the Messiah-Ox and patted his neck.

"Let her . . ." thought the Messiah-Ox. "Let her pat as much as her heart desires. If she'd only take off the red apron, all would be well." But, as Pisherl's mother, the angel Hannah-Deborah, says, "A fool brings trouble." The pregnant angel did not appreciate the Messiah-Ox's great forbearance. She patted and patted him. Suddenly she whispered in his ear, "The Messiah is coming."

The Messiah-Ox's entire huge body shuddered. "The Messiah is coming!" That meant that at any minute they would come to slaughter him. His body would be cut into pieces of meat. The meat would be cooked and the Zaddikim would devour his flesh appreciatively: "Ah . . . ah . . . a true taste of Eden." It made the ox wild. "The Messiah is coming . . . danger near . . . time to run . . . escape . . . escape from the slaughter knife."

The Messiah-Ox did not know (what is an ox supposed to know?) that this was just the pregnant angel Khasya's idea of a joke; there was still plenty of time left for him to graze on the Eden meadow before the Messiah was due to come. Suddenly, he bent his head and, catching the pregnant angel up on his horns, he began to run wildly.

My friend Pisherl and I set up a shout; we shouted with all of our strength. "The Messiah-Ox is running away; the Messiah-Ox is running away."

The three cowherds jumped up and started to whistle at the ox, and to chase him. The angel Khasya, quivering on his horns, set up such a yowling that young and old ran to see what had happened. They asked each other, "What is it, eh? What happened?"

"The Messiah-Ox hooked a pregnant angel on his horns and ran off."

"Let's chase him."

"Let's catch him. Let's bring him back."

"To hell with the angel. The Messiah-Ox is more important. What will the Zaddikim do without the Messiah-Ox if the Messiah should come?"

Now, a real chase began. Angels, young and old—anyone with wings—flew after the Messiah-Ox. The enraged animal ran like a thousand devils. No doubt the image of the knife that would slaughter him was before his eyes. He was running away from the great feast of his flesh that the Messiah would make for the Zaddikim. The pregnant angel twitched on his horns and waved her arms about, screaming and fainting at intervals, only to rouse herself to scream again.

The angel whispered in his ear, "The Messiah is coming"

We chased the Messiah-Ox. Before us flew the three cowherds; behind us, the angels, with or without beards. My friend Pisherl and I were the only children in pursuit. Some of the angels grew tired. They lost themselves in the crowd, panting, wiping the sweat from their wings, and finally they flew home.

"He's strong as iron, that Messiah-Ox."

"Did you ever see such running? Faster than the fastest Eden rabbit."

"The stupid female really scared him; she ought to be put in the courtyard of the synagogue and whipped until she promises never to play such practical jokes again."

That's the sort of thing the angels who returned to their homes were saying. Meanwhile, the Messiah-Ox continued to run away. We pursued him.

That Messiah-Ox did considerable damage in his flight. He ran across gardens, over newly sown fields where he trod down everything. He knocked over a couple of little angels who were playing ring-around-the-rosy. An old angel who was standing at the edge of a village playing a barrel organ was dealt such a blow that he turned several somersaults in the air before he fell in a dead faint from which he was revived only after the greatest difficulties.

"Pisherl! Do you see? He's heading westward, toward the border of the Christian Eden."

"I see, Shmuel-Aba. I see. May you live to tell me better news." It was beginning to get dark. The chase after the Messiah-Ox became more intense. If he was to be caught, it would have to be soon.

That was what we thought. But the Messiah-Ox had other ideas.

The pregnant angel quivering on his horns had no more strength left even to shriek. She was hoarse as a frog; her groans could barely be heard.

The Messiah-Ox's three cowherds were white as chalk. What would happen to them if, God forbid, the Messiah-Ox should cross the border into the Christian Eden? And by all indications, that was already happening. The bells of the Orthodox church were ringing, "Ding-dong. Ding-dong."

The leaps and dashes of the Messiah-Ox were so fierce that he was soon afoam with sweat. The border was very close. Already the Christian border guards, blond angels with blue eyes, could be seen. They wore huge boots and stood leaning on their pikes.

"Pisherl, what's going to happen?"

"A disaster," groaned my friend Pisherl. "A disaster, Shmuel-Aba."

The Messiah-Ox, the pregnant angel on his horns, crossed the border. Some of the Christian border guards tried to stop him, but he plunged on. Our angels, that is, the Jewish angels, drew up at the border. They could pursue the Messiah-Ox no farther. Or, to put it better, the Christian angels would have forbidden the pursuit.

Sad and shamefaced, we descended. We had no idea what to do, but stood looking after the Messiah-Ox as he disappeared in the distant fields.

An angel said, "Maybe they've caught him."

"What if they have," another angel retorted. "What good will it do us?"

"They're just as likely, God forbid, to make non-Kosher beef of him," a third angel observed.

"Our Messiah-Ox, God be praised, is fat enough. They can certainly make a feast of him."

"Our Zaddikim are going to be left with their tongues hanging out. They've spent a lifetime sharpening their teeth and now what—no Messiah-Ox."

"Bite your tongue," said the angel Henzl angrily.

"Where do you get that 'no Messiah-Ox'? He's here, all right. And how! All he's done is cross over into the Christian Eden—we have to see about getting him back." The angel Henzl smoothed his wispy beard importantly while he tried to think of some means of freeing the Messiah-Ox.

"What's to be done, Reb Henzl?" asked a short angel with a dense beard. "Advise us, Reb Henzl."

The angel Henzl made no reply. He went up to the Christian border guards and began to talk with them, partly in their language, partly in Yiddish, and partly with expressive gestures. "Our Messiah-Ox," the angel Henzl said, "crossed . . . made escape . . . your paradise."

"What?" asked the angel Vassil, the squadron leader of the Christian border guard.

"Our Messiah-Ox . . . to your paradise," said the angel Henzl once more; then he made signs to indicate someone running. The Christian border guard burst into laughter. He gave his mustaches a twitch and said fiercely, "Beat it, filthy Jew."

The angel Henzl shuddered. We stood around him, our wings lowered, as if we were lost. From the fields of the Christian Eden, we heard the sound of a "hurrah" and then laughter. Evidently some of the Christian angels had succeeded in catching the Messiah-Ox. We stood on our side of the border listening to the Christians' joy. Our hearts beat like crazy watches. The angel Hillel, the streetsweeper, sighed deeply. It was a sigh that could have been heard over a seven-mile radius.

The three barefooted cowherds stood about, looking as if they had been whipped. What were they to say when they were finally brought up on the carpet? ("So that's how you watched the Messiah-Ox, bastards." And the Zaddikim would spit full in their faces—and they would be right, too.

They just *had* to play cards, and while they played, the disaster happened.)

The laughter in the fields of the Christian Eden grew louder. "They're leading the Messiah-Ox toward the Christian stables. They're going to put that pious, Kosher animal near the same trough where they feed their pigs. Woe to them!"

The angel Henzl said, as if to no one in particular, "From bad to worse. They may even slaughter the Messiah-Ox with a non-Kosher knife. What will the holy Zaddikim say? How will the Great Feast look without the Messiah-Ox? Angels! Help. What's to be done? Suggest something."

"Suggest something! Easier said than done."

The night was pitch black. Our angels stood at the border, their wings drooping, not knowing what to do with themselves.

One of the barefooted cowherds said, "Do you know what? Let's light a fire meanwhile. We can warm up, and at the same time, we can consider how to break the news to Eden."

The idea of the fire pleased everyone. As I said, it was already late at night and we were shivering. The three cowherds gathered kindling and built a fire around which we sat.

Each of us put a finger to his forehead, thinking, trying to come up with a suggestion.

"What do you say, Pisherl?"

"What should I say, Shmuel-Aba? It's good and disgusting."

"Now *they* have the Messiah-Ox, and we have a fig for our pains, Pisherl."

"Then we'll have to do without the Messiah-Ox, Shmuel-Aba. When the Messiah comes, we can eat the Leviathan.

The flesh of the Leviathan is tastier than that of the Messiah-Ox."

The angel Henzl, who was listening to our conversation, flared up. Beside himself with rage, he delivered a speech that was continually interrupted by his swallowing the wrong way; but he went on.

"So, the punks are ready to leave the Messiah-Ox in the Christian Eden! Who says we'll leave the Messiah-Ox to 'them'? Have we herded him these thousands of years only to let them make a feast of him? Haven't they pigs enough over there? Do we have to leave them the Messiah-Ox as well? Let there be chaos; let there be darkness, do you hear? Let there be darkness, but let the Messiah-Ox be returned to us."

My friend Pisherl and I were frightened. We began to stammer, to apologize. "Don't be angry, Reb Henzl. We meant no harm, God forbid. We only wanted . . . we only said . . . you understand, Reb Henzl."

But the angel Henzl is difficult to calm once he gets worked up. He loomed above the fire and talked and talked, droning on like a mill. None of us understood a word.

Suddenly, with a flap of his wings, he extinguished the fire that had been flickering in the field and cried at the top of his voice, "Angels, up! Why are you crouched like crones before a fire? Let's rouse all of Eden. Let's make an uproar. Let us confront our disaster. Woe unto me, that I have lived to see this day."

We got up, spread our wings and flew. The angel Henzl went before us; his wings flapping fearfully, he shouted, "Like hell we'll let them have the Messiah-Ox. The Messiah-Ox is ours. We'll bring him back to our Eden by fair means—or foul."

X

The Turmoil over the Flight of the Messiah-Ox

THE NEWS that the Messiah-Ox had escaped set all Eden in a dither. One bird told another; one wind told another. In the morning, as we were coming back home, we found crowds of Zaddikim already in the streets. They were disturbed, gesticulating, unable to believe that it had really happened.

"Escaped . . . really . . . the Messiah-Ox?" the rabbi of Apt asked the rabbi of Lublin. "It can't be. Such a thing was never heard of."

The white head of the rabbi of Lublin trembled. One could see he was vexed. "The very birds are calling the news on the housetops and you go on with your, 'It's not possible.' "

The rabbi of Apt was tenacious. "Maybe it's only a dream, and all of this anxiety is for nothing."

The rabbi of Lublin shook his head. "A dream . . . a dream . . . If only it *were* a dream."

"No doubt they'll bring him back," said the rabbi of Apt, trying to console himself. "What do the saints in the

Christian Eden need the Messiah-Ox for? They prefer pig meat, and they have pigs in plenty."

The rabbi of Lublin accepted a pinch of snuff from the rabbi of Apt. He sniffed deeply, then sneezed aloud.

"You sneezed on the truth," said the rabbi of Apt, though he did not believe it himself.

I poked my friend Pisherl. "Where are the Messiah-Ox's three cowherds?" I asked. "They were with us just a while ago. Where did they disappear?"

"Why do you ask me? Can't you see for yourself that the cowherds are scared? The Zaddikim are furious with them for losing the Messiah-Ox. No doubt the cowherds are hiding somewhere in an attic."

We saw a cluster of people. In the middle stood the rabbi of Saddegura. His beard was disheveled; his eyes glittered. He was literally giving off sparks. "Where are they, the scoundrels? Where are the cowherds? They ought to be punished as they deserve. The little bastards ought to have their wings broken. They ought to be driven out of Eden; they, and their wives, and their children, and their children's children." The Zaddikim nodded their heads, agreeing with his bitter words.

We saw the rabbi of Horodenka, running breathlessly. His gabardine was unpinned and he had lost a slipper on the way. Now, he ran up to the crowd, panting, "What a calamity! What a grief! What will I do with the gold fork and knife I bought especially for the Great Feast? What a calamity!" The rabbi of Horodenka was a small man with a long beard. One could say without exaggeration that his beard reached to his knees. Pisherl could contain himself no longer and burst out laughing.

"Don't laugh, Pisherl," I said. "It's a sin."

"How can I help laughing? Just look at the little rabbi. One slipper on, the other off. God be praised, what an appetite he has." Our luck was that the Zaddikim were so engrossed in their discussion that none of them heard Pisherl's sly remarks.

"What's to be done? What's to be done?" the rabbi of Saddegura said, wringing his hands. "What sort of Great Feast can it possibly be without the Messiah-Ox?"

"We ought to cry woe . . . cry woe in the streets," the rabbi of Horodenka said heatedly. "Only think, such a thing has never happened before."

"This must be Satan's meddling," said the rabbi of Saddegura. "Where did the beast get the sense to think of running away?"

"Right. Right," the rabbi of Horodenka cried. "It's the work of Satan. Satan, may his name be cursed, has sneaked into Eden."

"We ought to inspect the *mezuzahs*," the rabbi of Zalishtchik suggested from the midst of the crowd. "Maybe a *mezuzah* has been defiled and that's the source of the whole calamity."

"Come," whispered Pisherl in my ear. "Let's leave these Galicians. Let them quarrel to their heart's content about spoiled *mezuzahs*. Let us fly on."

"Where, Pisherl?"

"I thought we might fly over and hear what the holy patriarchs have to say about the escape of the Messiah-Ox."

We left the crowd of Galician rabbis and flew in the direction of the Three Patriarchs' Allée where the patriarchs lived in their villas. On the way there, we passed a number of Zaddikim standing around in smaller or larger clusters. As we flew, we heard occasional words, "Messiah-Ox . . . escaped . . . cowherds . . . card-playing . . . to the Christian paradise . . . they must be punished . . . have their wings broken . . . what will the Messiah say?"

"The Messiah-Ox pulled off a real stunt, Pisherl. The

The Zaddikim stood in clusters

Zaddikim are at their wits' end. The rabbi of Koznetz has even forgotten to wear his fringed garment. . . ."

"And the grandfather of Shpoleh, Shmuel-Aba, has torn whole handfuls out of his beard; and how he beat his fists against his head, crying, 'My God, Jews. My God. What will we do if, God forbid, the Messiah should choose to come today?' "

"Tell me, Pisherl, where do these Zaddikim get their remarkable appetites?"

"You ask funny questions. Don't you know that the Zaddikim don't work? They never so much as put their hands in cold water. They go about all day long with nothing to do but to breathe the air; and it's said that the air is a great inducer of appetite."

We started down the Elijah-the-Prophet Boulevard. The morning sun covered the roofs with gold. The boulevard was empty. The richer angels were still asleep, and those Zaddikim who lived on the boulevard had gone to consult with the others about the calamity.

Shmaya, the policeman in the green uniform, stood at the corner, yawning, his wings drooping. He had his truncheon in his hand as usual, but this time he didn't know what to do with it. My friend Pisherl and I had a moment of pity for him. He stood so alone, so lost with nobody before whom to be important. We flew over his head, made several loop-the-loops hand in hand, and sang a little song that Pisherl had invented after the policeman had turned in his report about us and the goat:

> Shmaya, Shmaya, po-lice-man
> With his stick stuck in his hand,
> Stands upon the boulevard;
> Like a dummy, like a fool
> Wears a uniform of green.
> Entirely green, his uniform . . .
> Thinks he's great, thinks he's swell.

> Come and see, O come and see,
> You and him and her and me,
> Come snicker at the likes of him.

Shmaya the policeman turned red as a beet. When he spotted us, he waved his stick and, foaming at the mouth, started after us, his wings outspread. But we were lucky. Just at that moment, Elijah the Prophet, who was taking his first stroll of the day on his boulevard, made his appearance. "Shmaya, where are you flying, hah? Why are you so excited, Shmaya?"

Shmaya folded his wings again. It appeared that he was ashamed to tell Elijah that we had sung a satirical song at him. He saluted the old prophet with a smile. "Good morning, Reb Elijah. Have you heard, Reb Elijah, the Messiah-Ox has run off. All the Zaddikim in Eden are terribly upset about it, and you, Reb Elijah, are strolling about as if nothing had happened."

"I know. I know the Messiah-Ox has escaped and that the Zaddikim are all agog. Let them, let them boil away. They have something to stew about. They are fortunate in having sound teeth, God be praised, while I," and here the old prophet showed his gums, "as it turns out, have nothing with which to chew my portion of the Messiah-Ox."

We left the old prophet talking to the cop and flew on in the direction of the Three Patriarchs' Allée. "Do you know what I think, Shmuel-Aba?"

"How should I know what you think, Pisherl?"

"I think there must be considerable confusion among the patriarchs. I'm curious to see the patriarch Isaac. He's a great gourmand, our patriarch Isaac. He'd give you almost anything you can think of for a piece of good meat."

"How do you know that, Pisherl?"

Pisherl showed his astonishment. "Shmuel-Aba, have you forgotten what we learned in school? It's written clearly in the Bible that the patriarch Isaac loved Esau better because he regularly brought his father a portion of the meat from his hunting expeditions." Pisherl thought for a while. "And secondly, Shmuel-Aba . . . secondly, I myself saw how, one evening, when Isaac came to the meadow where the Messiah-Ox was grazing . . . how he brought with him a piece of chalk . . ."

"What was the chalk for, Pisherl?"

"He made a mark on the Messiah-Ox's right side, to designate which piece was to be his at the coming of the Messiah."

"But the patriarch Isaac is blind. How could he have known where to make the mark?"

"Leave it to him, Shmuel-Aba," replied Pisherl. "Blind as he is, he tapped about with his finger and found the fat spot. Then he made his mark."

We turned into the Bal-Shem Alley. It was a poverty-stricken alley; nevertheless, it was sunny. Here, the very poorest of the angels lived. They were so poor that there was only a single pair of wings to a household. When one member of the family took the wings to leave the house, the rest had to stay at home until he returned.

But in this alley, great wonder stories are told. Hungry as they are, they believe in miracles. Their stories are indeed remarkably lovely. But hunger does its work too, goading and goading, frequently interfering with their sleep.

Lovely little angels were playing in the alley. They were holding each other by the hand, turning in a circle and singing:

> Hi and ho and hmph
> Rivtsche is a nymph,
> She is a *grande dame*
> And Berkeh is her man.
> They fly about, these strollers,
> In wings of many colors.

All know them, both together—
In her hat, a feather;
He wears a silken top hat.
They have no children—that's flat
But wine and honey in a can
They've plenty, may they both be damned.

I pointed to the children playing in the Bal-Shem Alley. "Pisherl, the children are so poor and dirty, let's drop down and play with them a bit."

"God forbid," said Pisherl. "Have you forgotten, Shmuel-Aba? We're flying to the holy patriarchs to hear what they'll say about the Messiah-Ox."

"Only for a moment, Pisherl," I pleaded. "Let's just play a moment, then we'll fly on."

"No. Not this time. We've got to go. We'll play with them some other time," he said sternly. I had no choice but to give in. The alley curved and we had to fly carefully, slowly, to avoid scraping our wings.

No sooner had we left the Bal-Shem Alley and turned right than we recognized a familiar street. It was the Street of the Lovers of Israel. Here there lived Reb Moishe Laib of Sassov, Reb Velvl of Zbarash, and Reb Levi Jitzhak of Berditchev. These Zaddikim own small properties here. Behind every house, there's a cherry orchard. It's clear that they are not the richest of the Zaddikim; there are a great many who are much richer; still, things are not too bad for them. They have no anxieties about making a living. They spend their days praying that God will have pity on the children of Israel and make room for them in Eden.

We looked down and saw a man of middle height, wearing a simple gabardine, and, though it was really a warm day, his fur hat. He stood in the middle of the street, his head raised to the clouds, his arms lifted to the heavens. He was whispering.

*The rabbi of Berditchev stood with his
arms lifted to the heavens*

"It's the rabbi of Berditchev," my friend Pisherl said in my ear, "Reb Levi Jitzhak of Berditchev. No doubt, he's talking things over with the Almighty. In the hour of calamity, he always stands in the middle of the street with his Sabbath clothes on and weeps and pleads with God."

"Let's find out what Reb Levi Jitzhak is saying to God, Pisherl."

"All right, Shmuel-Aba," my friend agreed. "We'll drop down and listen to one of his prayers in Yiddish. But remember, we won't stay too long."

"Only one prayer, Pisherl. I want to hear one prayer and no more. We settled down quietly a few paces from the rabbi of Berditchev and listened. The rabbi of Berditchev stood, as I've said, with his arms outstretched to the heavens. He was pleading, and his pleas would have moved a stone:

> A good morning to you, O Lord of the Universe.
> I, Levi Jitzhak of Berditchev,
> Have come to you with a plea.
> Where is justice, O Lord of the Universe,
> And why do you plague your Zaddikim,
>   O Lord of the Universe?
>
> Is it true that they followed in your ways?
> You'll have to agree that they did . . . oh, yes.
> Is it true that they obeyed your laws?
> Once again, oh, yes.
> Did you not promise them Eden?
> Once again, Yes.
> And the Messiah-Ox and the Leviathan?
> And the red Messiah wine?
> Once more, the answer is yes.
>
> So where is the Messiah-Ox,
> Father in Heaven?

Escaped to the Christians,
Father in Heaven.
Then bring him back to us again,
Father in Heaven,
Don't make a mockery of the Great Feast,
Father in Heaven.

I don't plead on my account,
Father beloved,
But for your Zaddikim,
Father most faithful.

The rabbi of Berditchev waved back and forth, like a reed bent by the wind. There were tears in his voice, real tears.

"The rabbi of Berditchev must be a good man, Pisherl."

"A very good man, Shmuel-Aba. But let's keep going."

We flew on. Soon we were in the Three Patriarchs' Allée. By day, it was deserted; the benches that stood on both sides of the street were vacant. Only in the evening did the Allée begin to show life; then the betrothed couples appeared, whispering and kissing each other, vowing their love by the stars and the moon.

In the Three Patriarchs' Allée, it is always shadier than anywhere else. The birches along the roadside guard the Allée faithfully; not every sunbeam is privileged to get through.

At a distance, we discerned three Jews in fur hats who were walking along, waving their hands about. Judging by the movement of their shadows, we concluded that they were quarreling. As they drew nearer, we recognized the holy patriarchs walking rapidly.

The patriarch Isaac was in the middle. As always, he wore dark glasses. His speech was nervous, more nearly a shout than talk. "And I tell you, without the Messiah-Ox, Eden is not Eden. Whoever heard of a Jewish Eden without a Messiah-Ox? What sort of feast will the Great Feast be without so much as a morsel of meat? No feast at all, do you hear? No feast at all."

The patriarch Jacob, who was walking on the left, agreed with his father. He too thought that without the Messiah-Ox, the Great Feast would be an empty form. "Esau is lucky," Jacob said bitterly. "We, the Zaddikim of the Jewish Eden, put the Messiah-Ox out to pasture, and he, Esau, will get the joy of it. Father, that son of yours was always your favorite. Now you're being repaid. He'll eat up your portion of the Messiah-Ox as well."

"Don't even mention his name," the patriarch Isaac cried in a loud voice. "I don't want to hear his filthy name."

The patriarch Abraham pulled Jacob by the sleeve. "Jacob, why are you tormenting your father? If he's made a mistake, do you have to keep reminding him of it? He thought that Esau would straighten up and become a somebody, and so he cared for him. Had he known that he would turn into a gentile, he would have destroyed him root and branch."

The patriarch Jacob would not yield the point. He said that even if Esau had been—no matter what—Isaac would still have preferred him, just as long as Esau continued to bring him occasional tidbits to eat. His father (so Jacob argued) had always preferred his stomach to the Torah, and now he had . . .

The patriarch Isaac turned red with rage. A vein in his forehead swelled. He wanted to lunge at Jacob; to give it to him properly; to beat hell out of him.

But the patriarch Abraham interposed, scolding, "Here I've called a council together in the Great Synagogue and you're squabbling, ready to come to blows. Pfooh!"

Abraham's scolding helped calm Isaac down. He walked on silently, his head bowed.

"Did you hear, Shmuel-Aba? The patriarchs have called a council in the Great Synagogue. Let's go and listen, but be quick, Shmuel-Aba. If we get there in time we can hide so they won't drive us away."

"Good Pisherl. Let's go."

We flew off. Below us, the patriarchs looked like three dots. "Quickly, quickly," Pisherl urged, and we flew to the Great Synagogue.

At the synagogue, there were already a number of the Zaddikim. Naphthali, the caretaker of the synagogue, a man with a hump and a goat's beard, had flown from one villa to another, informing the Zaddikim that the patriarchs Abraham, Isaac, and Jacob were calling together a council. The Zaddikim had needed no urging to attend. Each one took a walking-stick in hand and went at once.

My friend Pisherl and I went into the synagogue. No one noticed us, since they were all engrossed in themselves and in the escape of the Messiah-Ox. Hiding behind a bench that stood on the south side, we watched and listened.

The synagogue filled up. There was no longer even standing room, and yet more and more late Zaddikim pressed in. They pushed and shoved, elbowing each other, treading on each other's corns, until finally they got in. The air was so thick that we—my friend Pisherl and I— could hardly breathe. "What good is all this going to do us?" I asked Pisherl.

"Shhh—Shmuel-Aba." Pisherl put his hand over my mouth. "They'll hear us and throw us out."

Abraham, the oldest of the patriarchs, appeared on the podium. With the thumb of his right hand stuck in his waistband, he waved his left hand over the heads of the audience. "A great disaster has befallen us, friends," he began. "The Messiah-Ox has escaped; and not merely escaped as occasionally happens with an ox, but he's run off to the Christian Eden. Now, where did the Messiah-Ox get the intelligence to escape?—that's a question that cannot be answered at this time, my friends.

"At this time, we need to consider . . . to investigate . . . to find an idea that will help us bring him back, back to his place in the Jewish Eden." The audience set up a commotion. A man with a grizzled beard began thrusting about with his elbows, pushing closer and closer to the podium.

"I have a parable," he cried. "Friends, I have a parable just suited to this occasion—a precious parable, with a golden moral. Once upon a time, there was a king who had three—"

"No need for parables, Preacher of Dubno," cried voices in the audience. "We need advice, not parables." But the Dubno Preacher was stubborn. He shouted everyone down and pushed his way, with all his force, toward the podium.

"You will regret it, gentlemen. It's a precious parable. The moral is a golden moral. Once there was a king—" The Preacher of Dubno might have succeeded in telling his parable if a drum roll had not been heard at the door.

A Zaddik cried out, "King Solomon has driven up. He's just getting out of his carriage." For a moment the synagogue grew still, then the buzzing began again.

"King Solomon . . . the wisest man . . . he has the brains of a prime minister . . . fool . . . a king is greater . . . the king is a lord, and a minister is no more than a servant." Quarrels broke out. There were cries of "oaf," "fool," and other such nicknames. Suddenly, the voice of the synagogue caretaker was heard at the back. "Make way for King Solomon."

King Solomon thrust his way toward the podium at once. He was sweating like a beaver and wiping his forehead with a silk handkerchief.

The synagogue grew hushed. Solomon's tall, broad-shouldered figure, his fox-red beard, his sharp, intelligent eyes commanded respect. He spoke softly, unhurriedly. "As soon as I heard the full story, I wasted no time, but sent a letter off to the Christian saints . . . if you know what I mean . . . I wrote to them about this and that and how much would they want for the return of the Messiah-Ox . . . if you know what I mean. We are ready to do business, I wrote . . . though we can do without the Messiah-Ox . . . he's not so very necessary to us and—"

At this point, the patriarch Isaac could contain himself no longer. He leaped from his seat and cried, "What do you mean we don't need him? We *need* him. Without the Messiah-Ox . . . where does he get off writing 'them' that we can do without the Messiah-Ox?"

King Solomon smiled wisely and reassured the outraged Isaac. "It's only a manner of speaking, if you know what I mean, Reb Isaac. One mustn't let them know that the Messiah-Ox is the apple of our eye. If they knew, they would ask for his weight in gold . . . if you know what I mean." Putting his finger to his forehead, he added slyly, "That's diplomacy, Reb Isaac. Diplomacy. One needs to understand it . . . if you know what I mean."

All the Zaddikim nodded, agreeing that King Solomon was right, that he was indeed a wise man—if you turned Eden upside-down, you wouldn't find his match.

"So . . . I . . . if you know what I mean," continued Solomon, "so I wrote a letter inquiring how much they wanted. I sent the letter off with one of my postal pigeons. I estimate that we'll have a reply on the morning of the day after tomorrow."

A commotion began down below. "Where does he get off writing without our knowledge? We might at least have been informed of the contents of the letter. After all, we have a small stake in the matter . . ."

King Solomon always hated back talk. Drawing himself up to his full height, his beard flaming, his eyes ablaze, he roared, "Attention!" with the voice of a lion.

The Zaddikim stopped in their tracks, like soldiers before their commanding officer. There was not so much as the flicker of an eyelid. They stood this way for some fifteen minutes until King Solomon said, "Enough. Now you can go home. And when I get a reply from the Christian Eden, I'll let you know." He stepped down from the podium and pushed his way through the crowd. Outside, his gilded coach was waiting.

No sooner was Solomon gone than a dispute broke out. It was argued that King Solomon ought to have consulted with the Zaddikim. Wise though he might be, he was, after all, only one man, and they were numerous. And though the Zaddikim might not be as wise as he, still, their numbers counted for something.

"He's always behaved like this. He's always done just what he wanted, and paid about as much attention to us as to the cat . . ."

"Pfooh! Pfooh! Jews, you're talking against a king . . . against a king," cried a small Zaddik with a sparse beard.

A way was made for the holy patriarchs. They left the synagogue and went home. "Then we may expect an answer on the morning of the day after tomorrow," said the patriarch Isaac.

The patriarch Abraham comforted him, "Don't worry. The reply will be favorable."

"May your wish pass from your mouth to God's ear, Father. And amen," sighed the patriarch Isaac. The patriarchs continued on their way.

XI

Our Mission

SEVERAL DAYS went by, but there was no reply. The Zaddikim became extremely nervous. At night, they said prayers; by day, they peered their eyes out, watching for the postal pigeon that was to bring the reply; but there was no pigeon nor any reply to be seen.

"They're making dreadful fun of us," said the patriarch Isaac. "Woe unto my old age that I should have lived to see this . . ."

"Your Esau," Jacob taunted him, "your favorite son. He knows that his father is dying for a piece of Messiah-Ox—and there is none."

"Still talking back to your father." The patriarch Abraham turned his dark eyes on him. "Where is 'Honor thy father . . . ,' Jacob?"

Jacob's wife, Rachel, ran into the house. She was breathless. From under her wig there peeped strands of her own hair. She was still slender and lovely. No sooner did Jacob see her than he became a different man. His eyes lighted up; he ran to her, caressed her head, and said, "Why are you running so, darling? May your loveliness be blessed."

157

Rachel looked up at him affectionately and said, "I met Esther on the street. She still carries herself as if she were a queen. A silk dress in the middle of the week, a gold ring on every finger, a strand of pearls around her neck. May such things be said about every Jewish daughter. I pretended I didn't see her and wanted to pass her by. I'm not fond of the beauty. But she stopped me and said, 'I want to tell you . . . a fast is what's needed. If you want the Messiah-Ox back, the best remedy will be a fast.' "

The patriarch Abraham said, "That's right. She's right. A fast must be declared in Eden."

In short, a fast was declared. Everyone fasted. The Zaddikim became so weak that they could hardly keep on their feet, but there was still no sign of the postal pigeon.

A strange thing happened in the course of those fast days. The angel Shimon-Ber, as was his custom, got drunk and beat his wife to within an inch of her life. He dragged her by the hair through Eden, raving in his drunken voice, "What do you need the Messiah-Ox for, Zaddikim? You need an animal? Here! I've got one for you. I'll let you have her for a bottle of ninety-six."

They tried to calm him down; to explain to him that the angel he was dragging by the hair was not an animal, but his own wife who was in her seventh month. He would have none of it, but kept up his continual shouting. "A half pint of vodka and the creature is yours, Zaddikim."

The Eden police were called. Several angels in green uniforms came flying and at last, with great difficulty, were able to bind Shimon-Ber. They took him off to sober up in the Eden jail. His wife was revived only after the greatest difficulties. She was taken home more dead than alive.

"He has to choose just such dreadful days as these in which to get drunk," the Zaddikim grumbled. "That Shimon-Ber ought to have been a Christian and not a Jewish angel."

Finally, on the twelfth day, there was news that the postal pigeon had returned, bringing a letter from the Christian Eden. King Solomon had the letter. Though no one as yet knew its contents, there was great joy. People kissed each other in the streets, tears in their eyes.

On that very day, King Solomon called together a council. He read the reply to everyone:

> To the most worthy and well-born saints of the Jewish Eden: Our reply to your letter is thus and thus. Your Messiah-Ox crossed our borders without passport or visa. According to the laws of our Eden he must be punished for the damage he created with six months at hard labor and half a pound of hay as a daily food allowance.
>
> As for the pregnant angel whom he brought with him on his horns, we stand ready to return her to you. But the infant, born in our territory, will be baptized and will remain with us.
>
> We are prepared to send the Messiah-Ox to you just as soon as he has served his sentence and worked off the damages assessed against him.

When King Solomon had read the letter, there was weeping and wailing in the Jewish Eden. Zaddikim ran about like poisoned mice, unable to find a resting place. They wrung their hands and wailed in anguish, "Who ever heard of such a thing? Six months in jail! Half a pound of hay per day. To work out damages . . . They'll send the Messiah-Ox back to us nothing but skin and bones."

The wives of the Zaddikim squealed, "Such a thing hasn't been heard of since the world began. To take a Jewish infant angel and baptize him. Woe to us who have lived to see such a thing."

Only one person did not lose his head. That was King Solomon. He wrote a second letter making various proposals, in the course of which he flattered the Christian saints. The wise king knew that flattery was a fine remedy against opposition.

The answer to the second letter came three days later. King Solomon read it before the chief of the Zaddikim.

> To the most honorable King Solomon, the wisest of the wise. This is to inform you that we have received your letter. We have agreed to accept a diamond from your crown as payment for the damages caused by the Messiah-Ox. But the Ox will still have to serve his sentence for crossing the border without passport or visa. The law is the law; but to show that we want to meet you halfway, we have imposed only a three months' sentence. As for the infant born on our soil, we have already baptized him and named him Peter. The newly delivered mother is at your disposition. You may have her back whenever you like.

"Three months on jail food, and that's the end of the Messiah-Ox," wailed the patriarch Isaac.

"A Jewish infant, baptized," cried Mother Sarah, wringing her hands. She was joined in her sorrow by Rebecca, Leah, and Rachel.

"What a calamity; how shameful. And all on account of the stupidity of the cowherds," the Zaddikim cried.

King Solomon wrote a third letter, agreeing that the Messiah-Ox deserved to be punished, but he argued that three months was too long. Furthermore, three months on prison food would kill the animal; he proposed therefore, that they, the Christian saints, should permit two Jewish cowherds to look after the Messiah-Ox for the time of his incarceration. "We stand ready," King Solomon wrote, "to send several wagons of hay so that he will have enough to eat." As for the baptized infant angel—he would let that matter drop. "Regarding the Messiah-Ox, I await a prompt reply."

The postal pigeon took the letter and delivered it to the Christian Eden. An answer came at the end of three days. Again, King Solomon read the letter to the Zaddikim. Once again, the Christian saints made no difficulties. They agreed to let the Jewish Eden send over two angels who would look after the Messiah-Ox until he had done his time, but they warned that cowherds were not to be sent. If the Messiah-Ox were to see a Jewish cowherd, he would run wild again. The best idea would be for the Zaddikim to send two little angels whom the Messiah-Ox would trust. As for the Ox's punishment, the Christian saints would cut his sentence to six weeks. That much time, he would have to serve. Regarding the diamond, they said that King Solomon could send it along with the little angels who would be sent to look after the Messiah-Ox.

This letter pleased everyone. "The saints of the Christian Eden can be talked to. One can see that from this letter."

"Well. Whom shall we send?" the patriarch Abraham inquired, stroking his dignified beard. The Zaddikim considered the matter, suggesting first one and then another. Finally, someone mentioned Pisherl as "a bright little angel who knows what's what."

"And the second one?" someone inquired.

"The second one? I think the second one might be . . ."

"Well, who? Let's hear who? There's someone who keeps on saying 'the second one . . . the second one . . .' and there's no name to be heard," murmured others.

"I think the second should be Pisherl's friend, Shmuel-Aba. They're very fond of each other . . . like two brothers. And as for Shmuel-Aba, he's as bright as they come."

In short, it was decided that I and my friend Pisherl

should fly to the Christian Eden to look after the Messiah-Ox. We were told to go to Zaidl, the Eden photographer, to get passport photos made.

We went off happily. Zaidl, the Eden photographer, was delighted to see us and pinched each of us on the cheek. "How good that you've come. I'll read you the Purim play I've just written."

Zaidl, the Eden photographer, was a long-haired angel who wore glasses. He had one weakness—he wrote a new Purim play every week and would read it to anyone he could catch.

We explained that we had come to be photographed and that we had no time now to listen because we were flying on a mission to the Christian Eden. When, with God's help, we got back again, he could read to us as much as he liked.

The angel Zaidl turned glum. He very much wanted to read his play, but there was nothing to do except put it off until we returned. "By then," he promised us, "I'll have six new Purim plays. Remember to come, lads. You'll enjoy yourselves."

He photographed us and had the pictures ready on the spot. We went to the police department where our passports were made out. With them in hand, we went to say good-by to Pisherl's parents.

Pisherl's mother wiped her eyes with her apron. "Be careful, Pisherl. Don't catch cold on the way, God forbid."

And Pisherl's father, Shlomo-Zalman, the patch-tailor, told us sternly, "Don't let the Christian angels talk you into anything. Don't eat any pork, do you hear?" He gave us a headful of similar *don't's* and ended finally on a hiccup, "And don't forget you are Jewish angels, and that it's an honor to be an angel in the Jewish Eden."

We promised him everything he wished. Pisherl's

The angel Zaidl, the Eden photographer

mother gave us several buckwheat cookies to take along, and we said good-by.

"Fly in good health and come back well," they cried after us.

"Now, Shmuel-Aba, we have to fly to King Solomon's to get the diamond. From there, we'll go straight on to the border." We rose up higher and higher into the air. It was something of a long trip to King Solomon's estates, but we were so excited by the journey that we didn't even notice the passage of time.

"Shmuel-Aba, do you see there, the building with the golden roof? That's King Solomon's palace."

We dropped down. The angels who guarded the palace had been told of our coming and they let us in at once.

We approached a silver stream. Shulamith sat at its edge, her bare feet in the water. She was catching fish in a golden net. "If she only knew that we saw her at King David's palace. What do you suppose she'd do?"

"We're on an important mission, Shmuel-Aba. And you have to think up stupidities."

We crossed the wooden bridge. Behind us, we could hear Shulamith singing.

> With you together,
> My beloved,
> I would go
> As deep as Hell.
>
> How grim, my dear,
> To be in Hell
> Where prayers are useless
> And tears as well.
>
> Tears are no solace,
> No solace is prayer,
> But a song of true love
> May comfort us there.

We turned off to one side and Shulamith's song became fainter and fainter. Already, it was almost out of earshot. My friend and I were very fond of songs and at any other time we would have lingered for an hour or two to listen, but now, when we were getting ready to fly off on such a long journey, we had no time.

We found King Solomon standing in the courtyard. He was wearing a silk robe and slippers. His crown glittered on his head. He was engaged in conversation with a cocky little rooster. As is well known, King Solomon understood the language of the beasts, the birds, and the fowl. We saw for ourselves how he put questions to the rooster and how the rooster replied, but we were not able to understand the answers.

We were becoming impatient. Who knew how long they might stand talking this way; and we had such a long journey before us.

Pisherl poked me, "Well Shmuel-Aba."

"What Pisherl?"

"Let's approach him."

We approached and bowed before the king. The king interrupted his conversation with the rooster.

"Your majesty, we've come for the diamond. We're flying to the Christian Eden to look after the Messiah-Ox." King Solomon took his crown off and removed the diamond from it. He played with it for a moment or two. The diamond sparkled, dazzling our eyes.

"Take it, lads. And see that you don't lose it. It's an expensive gem—worth twenty-five thousand korona."

We took the diamond, promising the king that we would guard it like the eyes in our heads. He waved his hand, indicating that we could fly off.

"We're off, Shmuel-Aba."

We spread our wings and flew in the direction of the

King Solomon was engaged in conversation with a rooster

border. We arrived there in the evening between twilight and evening prayers. Bells were ringing in all the churches. The twilight, the festive singing, and the sound of the bells appeared strange and foreign to us. We pressed closer, fearful lest we lose one another.

An angel in a blue uniform with two crosses on his wings examined our passports. Two other angels in gray uniforms searched us to see whether, God forbid, we might not be smuggling any Talmuds in. The Talmud is regarded as a most terrible thing in the Christian Eden.

The border formalities lasted more than an hour but they found nothing on us and our passports were in order.

The angel in the blue uniform led us to a huge iron gate. He knocked three times and demanded entry. A voice that we recognized at once as belonging to an old man was heard on the other side of the gate. "Who knocks there?" it inquired.

"Saint Peter, it's me, the angel Theodore, the border guard. I've brought you a couple of little kikes from the Jewish Eden." We could hear a key being inserted in a lock. The lock groaned and the huge, heavy door swung open.

A little old man with a long white beard and twinkly eyes stood before us. He was baldheaded. In his right hand, he held the Eden key. He looked us over for a bit. The cross on his chest was of pure gold. The angel in the blue uniform saluted. Saint Peter made the sign of the cross over him and told him to go. The border had been left unguarded long enough.

The old gatekeeper told us to follow him. We entered and Saint Peter shut the gate again, saying, "No doubt you're hungry from your long trip. Rest here for a while. Tomorrow morning, a messenger will come to take you to the prison stables where the Messiah-Ox is."

Not far from the gate, there was a house where Saint Peter lived. It was an extremely dark night and a votive candle was already burning in his window. "You don't need to be afraid, lads. Nothing bad will happen to you. Come with me." He went before us and we followed. I don't know about Pisherl, but *my* heart was beating loudly.

We entered the house. It was roomy, and there were icons hanging from every wall. There was a table in the middle of the room and the old fellow told us to sit down.

We seated ourselves at the table. He gave each of us a hunk of black bread and some cheese, smiling at us meanwhile. "You won't eat any pork, eh? If you only knew the taste of a bit of pork. But then, you're stubborn. You don't want any. A splendid food, a bit of pork. Even your teacher at Hebrew school tells you to *khazer* well."*

We didn't reply, but ate our bread and cheese. After our journey, we were really terribly hungry. The old fellow inquired about the Zaddikim. He particularly wanted to know whether our patriarchs were well or having troubles of any kind.

Pisherl said that everything was in good order. Except for the problem with the Messiah-Ox, all was well.

"Tomorrow, you'll be taken to the Messiah-Ox," Saint Peter said. "But see that you don't go wandering off from your quarters. And don't go flying around our paradise. Among us, Jewish angels are not liked. See that you behave yourselves. Be discreet, and you won't get your wings broken."

We promised not to irritate anyone. If only we were not picked on, all would be well.

"The best thing," the old fellow advised us, "would be

* The pun turns on the similarity between the two words *khazir,* meaning pork (or pig), and *khazer,* meaning to repeat (as for a lesson).

to mind your own business. If our saints should be on their way to prayer, don't let them catch a glimpse of you. If you see a procession, get out of sight so no one will see hide nor hair of you."

"Some mess," I thought. "We'll have to hide to keep from being seen. What's the point of the whole thing if we're not to see anything, no matter what?"

Pisherl and I exchanged glances. We understood each other. Evidently he too had regrets for the entire affair. Old Peter's eyes began to close. He led us to a separate little room where there were no icons. "You'll spend the night here, fellows. And if you should have to do an 'angelic' thing, you can do it through the window."

The old man went back to his room. Pisherl and I remained by ourselves looking at each other with mournful eyes. I went to the window and looked out. The sky was clouded over; there was the smell of rain. We were not very light of heart. We thought of home and prayed to God that the weeks would pass quickly. There was a streak of lightning outside that illuminated our room for a moment. Then there was a second flash. Thunder grumbled and grumbled until, with a crash, it fell to the ground. We blessed ourselves aloud. In the other room, we could hear Saint Peter snoring.

"Shmuel-Aba?"

"What is it, Pisherl?"

"Let's go to sleep. One gets through the night more quickly asleep."

We undressed and went to bed but could not sleep. The lightning and thunder wouldn't permit it. In the Jewish Eden, we had often experienced such nights, but here, in a strange country, far away from all we knew, the stormy night was more fearful.

"Pisherl?"

"What, Shmuel-Aba?"

"Let's tell stories. If we tell stories, the time will pass more quickly."

We huddled closer and Pisherl began to tell the story of a beggar and a prince; but the thunder would not let him finish. Finally, he had to break off his story in the middle. We tried covering ourselves with the bedclothes, but that was no help. We jumped out of bed.

Pisherl opened the window and went outside where he stood in his nightshirt, lightning flashing around him. Anyone who has not seen my friend Pisherl illuminated by lightning doesn't know what loveliness is. "Shmuel-Aba," Pisherl said, "jump down through the window, Shmuel-Aba."

For a while, I hesitated, then I jumped. Just at that moment, the rain poured down and we got wet as fish. Our wings grew so heavy we could hardly lift them.

We went back into the room, water pouring from our heads and wings. The floor turned wet. We crawled back into bed and huddled close against each other, trying to get warm. Outside, the rain continued to pour down.

"Pisherl, do you hear?"

"What, Shmuel-Aba?"

"What the rain says." It was going "tap . . . tap . . . drop . . . bzsh . . . tap . . . a-drop . . . bzsh. . . ."

Our arms wound around each other, we fell asleep. In my dream, King Solomon was conversing with the rooster. I understood every word they said to each other. "How are you, rooster? And how are your thousand wives?" the king asked.

"Thank you so much, king, for your kind question. My wives are laying eggs and cackling, and, the Lord be praised, they are well. And how are your thousand wives, king?"

"Without meaning to be sinful, still . . . do you know something, rooster, among my thousand wives there isn't one who is entirely right." King Solomon grew thoughtful.

"If that's the case, O king, I'm luckier than you. My wives are doing fine. Not one of them is barren. If you want my advice, king, take a few more wives. A good one is bound to show up."

"Rooster, maybe you're right. So long as there's life, one ought to keep looking. A good one may turn up." Suddenly, a strange thing happened. As I watched, King Solomon turned into a rooster. His comb was fiery red. He flapped his wings and flew up to the top of a fence. "Cock-a-doodle-do."

At this cry, I woke up. "A curious dream," I thought. Outside, it was already dawn. The Eden roosters were crowing. My friend was still asleep. Evidently, he was very tired. He had his right hand over his heart and he was smiling. Asleep as he was, he was very lovely. Unable to restrain myself, I kissed him on the forehead.

I crept quietly out of bed. It seemed a pity to wake him. I went to the window and looked out. After last night's rain, the earth was fresh. The grass smelled . . . it was a delight to the soul. The birds in the trees were singing.

"Lovely is thy creation, O Lord of the Universe," I whispered. "But I can't understand why you needed three Edens. Wouldn't it have been better to have one for everyone? No passports; no visas; no quarrels." My heretical thought frightened me. "Some nerve," I scolded myself. "You are going to teach wisdom to the Lord of the World, Shmuel-Aba? He has more wisdom in the least fingernail of his smallest finger than you'll ever have in your entire body."

The sun rose in the east. It was huge, brilliant. One

golden ray fell on Pisherl's nose and tickled it so long that he finally woke up.

"Good morning, Pisherl."

Pisherl rubbed his eyes. He seemed for an instant to have forgotten where he was. Then he jumped out of bed. We washed ourselves and said our morning prayers. Our spirits were considerably improved.

We went into Saint Peter's room. The old man wasn't there. He had gone to church to say his prayers. There was a pitcher of milk on the table. We drank the milk and ate some black bread. In the distance, we could hear the ringing of bells.

Peter came home. Seeing us, he smiled good humoredly and gave each of us a pinch on the cheek. "Well, boys. Have you prayed this morning?" he inquired.

"Of course we have. Do you suppose we'd have eaten without saying our morning prayers? How would that have looked?"

"All right, all right," the old man smiled. The angel who is to take you to the Messiah-Ox is expected at any minute. Remember, behave yourselves and all will be well."

We looked at him and swore to behave ourselves. He nodded his head, satisfied. Once at the table, he crossed himself and began to eat. As we watched him, we felt ourselves growing more comfortable with him. The clock on the wall struck seven.

XII

cAnyella

SAINT PETER wiped his lips, stroked his beard, and asked us to give him the diamond out of King Solomon's crown. Pisherl handed it over. Peter examined it from all sides, smacking his lips all the while. "A rare diamond. A diamond of a diamond. A diamond like this is worth—I don't myself know how much!"

The old fellow opened a drawer from which he took a sheet of paper and wrote out a receipt—a declaration that he had received the diamond. Pisherl put the receipt away. Peter cleared the table. The clock on the wall struck nine.

We heard a knock on the door, and before the old saint could say "come in" the door was opened and there entered a tall, broad-shouldered angel with gray piercing eyes. He bowed before the old apostle, flapped his wings three times and said, "I've come for the little kikes. My name is Dmitri; I'm going to take them to the Messiah-Ox." He cast a baleful look at us. His piercing eyes and his tightly twirled mustaches made it clear that he was an enemy of the Jews—a real anti-Semite.

Old Peter whispered something into his ear. We stood to

one side, trembling. The angel Dmitri gave his mustaches a twirl and with a venomous smile, he said, "Let's go, Jew-boys."

We had no choice but to go with him. The old saint accompanied us to the door.

We took off. The angel Dmitri flew before us, waving his strong, huge wings and singing,

> Jew, Jew,
> Foolish Jew,
> No more Sabbath
> Coat for you.

We despised his song, but we could say nothing. We had to listen and be silent. I could see the tears in Pisherl's eyes. The angel Dmitri kept looking back. Our wings were young and weaker than his, but he was angry because we "flew like dying chickens."

He kept tormenting us, making fun of the way we spoke: "Mommy . . . Daddy . . . Mommy . . . Daddy . . ." God only knows what we endured in the course of our flight with this monster. We cursed the days of our lives and wished our wings had been broken before ever we had started on our journey.

At evening, we alighted near a wood. At our right was the prison stable with its barred windows. An angel with a sword marched back and forth before it, guarding the prisoner. The angel Dmitri led us up to the angel on guard and said something to him in a language we didn't understand. He kept pointing to us all the while. The angel on watch said, "Good," and Dmitri bade him farewell. He spread his wings and flew away. We could hear his song for a long while, "Jew, Jew, foolish Jew . . ."

The guard opened a heavy iron gate with a huge key. We went into the prison stable and saw our Messiah-Ox where he lay bound in chains. He was thin as a rail. If we had not known it was he, we would under no circumstances have recognized him.

Pisherl went up to him and caressed him. The Messiah-Ox looked up at him with huge, sorrowful eyes. "Now what did you accomplish by running away," Pisherl said. "A silly female angel makes a joke, and you go running off."

The Messiah-Ox seemed to understand my friend's scolding. He had a look of regret in his eyes. Pisherl consoled him, continuing his caresses. "Only a few more weeks, Messiah-Ox, and we'll go back to the Jewish Eden. You know, we've been sent especially to look after you; and later, we'll take you back home. And next time you'll know better. There'll be such joy when you get back, just you wait and see."

I too went up to him and caressed him; I told him how the Eden meadows longed for him. Since his escape, the grass on the meadow has been strangely sad. The crickets no longer sang, and the butterflies fluttered around like orphans, unable to find a resting place.

"But when you come back," Pisherl said, "everything will be all right again. The Eden meadow will blossom, the crickets will sing, and the butterflies will know that the Eden meadow is their home again."

The guard gestured to us. We understood that he wanted us to leave. Time was up for today. We said goodby to the Messiah-Ox, promising to come tomorrow, and left the prison stable. The guard locked the gate again, and we stood outside, not knowing what to do, where to go, or where we would spend the night.

"Shmuel-Aba?"

"What, Pisherl?"

"How will it all end, Shmuel-Aba?"

"May I know as much about evil as I do the answer to *that*."

The sky grew dark. The stars sparkled over the wood; they were the same stars as at home, and yet, they seemed very strange.

When it was quite dark, we saw an old fellow with a long white beard approaching. He carried a sack on his shoulders. I stared at him and would have sworn it was the prophet Elijah.

Evidently, Pisherl thought so too. He poked me and whispered, "See, Shmuel-Aba. The prophet Elijah."

"Pisherl, since when does the prophet Elijah wear a cross on his breast?"

The old fellow came up to us. The guard waved his sword and shouted, "Halt." We came to a stop, like soldiers. The old fellow patted our heads, smiling gently and good-humoredly. "So you are the little Jewish angels . . . good . . . I'm Saint Nicholas. I'll show you where you'll be staying for a while. In the meantime, here's a little present. Go on, take it; take it."

He untied his sack and gave Pisherl a leaden soldier, and me a rooster made of tin. The old fellow spoke Hebrew, which pleased us tremendously. He tied his sack again and threw it over his shoulders. "Come on, fellows." He went before us and we followed, feeling very comfortable with him. As we entered the wood, the old angel lighted his lantern.

We went on slowly. By the light of the lantern, we could see the squirrels jumping from tree to tree. We could hear the night birds calling each other. A doe ran across our path. In the distance, we could hear the splashing of water.

The old saint looked back at us frequently and smiled. He said, "You're tired, fellows. Soon, soon, and we'll be at the forest ranger's. That's where you'll stay until the Messiah-Ox has served his sentence."

He was right. We were indeed tired. We had been flying all day with that monster, the angel Dmitri; but we went on, just managing to keep on our feet. The sound of water was getting closer and closer. At the very edge of a river, there stood a small wooden house. The old saint stopped, put his lantern down and knocked, "Open, Ivan. It's me, Saint Nicholas."

The door opened. Ivan the forest ranger came out. He was an angel of middle height with short strong wings.

Saint Nicholas said, "These two little Jewish angels will stay with you, Ivan. See that you take care of them. They won't eat our food, so give them uncooked milk from an earthen vessel and black bread." The old angel bade us farewell and went away. He was soon lost among the forest trees.

We went into the house. On the walls there hung holy pictures. The river could be seen from the window. The forest ranger angel Ivan looked us over from head to toe. He was amazed, and hardly knew what to say. Finally, he made a movement with his hand and said, "Never mind."

The door of the second room opened and a girl angel with blond braids and blue eyes came in. The forest ranger said something to her in a language we did not understand, but we gathered that she was called Anyella.

She went back into the other room. After a short interval, she was back, carrying fresh milk and black bread. We settled ourselves greedily to eat, slurping the milk, munching the fresh rye bread with the greatest joy. The forest ranger angel took his gun down from the wall. He went up to Anyella, kissed her on the forehead and went off to spend the night guarding the forest. We were left alone with the little girl angel, the forest ranger's daughter. She kept herself busy around the house, tidying up and singing like a canary all the while.

I liked her a lot, that Anyella. Her slightest movement was a delight; but Pisherl was in a transport of joy. He called me aside and whispered, "How beautiful, Shmuel-Aba. I've never seen anything like it. Let her just say the word and I'll stay here, in the Christian Eden. I could look at her from morning till night."

At these words from my friend, I became terribly disturbed. I said to myself, "Those are the very words spoken by the infatuated couples in the Three Patriarchs' Allée." My heart ached. I was afraid that my friend was already lost. "But you're a Jewish angel, Pisherl, and she is a Christian. The two words don't rhyme, Pisherl."

My friend was instantly saddened. I had reminded him of something that hurt.

Outside there were the sounds of the forest and the water. In the house, Anyella went from place to place. Pisherl could not take his eyes from her. I pulled him by the right wing, "Come on, Pisherl. Let's go outside for a bit."

He followed me, in a trance. We sat down at the river's edge. The moon appeared from behind a cloud. Pisherl sighed.

"The real symptoms," I thought. "No sooner does the moon show itself than he sighs. Any minute now and he'll begin to write poetry. That little blond angel has bewitched him."

Pisherl was silent. I listened to the sound of the water. Suddenly, there was a burning sensation on my left wing. It was my friend Pisherl's tear. "God be with you, Pisherl. Why are you crying?"

Without answering my question, he put an arm around me and began to sing:

> Dear heart, since I have seen you
> Keeping your father's house,
> I've sworn a vow to love you
> Truly, I confess.
>
> There's no place I can find, dear,
> To rest, since you appeared.
> Through the streets I wander—
> I know I shall go mad.

This was another of Siomkeh's songs. Pisherl did not yet have one of his own; he might still be saved. "Let's get away, away from here, while there is still time; while your love is still only a spark. Once it turns into fire, it'll be too late, Pisherl."

"What, Shmuel-Aba?"

"Let's fly away from here. Quickly. This moment."

"What about the Messiah-Ox, Shmuel-Aba?"

What could I say to that? We had been sent here to look after the Messiah-Ox, and to bring it back home. I thought for a while, and then I said, "Anyella isn't very pretty. Your sister Ettl is much prettier, and other Jewish angels are prettier still."

My friend sighed. "You're speaking nonsense, Shmuel-Aba. Anyella is beautiful. It isn't right to malign an angel, even if she is a foreigner."

"He's caught in the trap," I thought. "He's speaking high sounding words. May God help him; I don't know if *I* can."

We heard Anyella, who was standing at the open window, calling, "Hey, boys."

Pisherl trembled. We got up and went into the house.

Anyella made signs to us to show us where to sleep; she led us into a separate room, and then went off to her own chamber. We went to bed. Pisherl talked continually in his sleep, keeping me awake. In the morning, when we got up, Anyella gave us milk and black bread.

The forest ranger angel was already home, sleeping and snoring. Anyella drove the goats out of the stable. My friend Pisherl and I flew off to the prison stable where the Messiah-Ox lay. We wanted to see to it that he was fed on time and not tormented.

After our arrival, the Messiah-Ox's portion of hay was increased. He began to improve, to put on a little weight. With every gram added to his weight, I felt a proportionate joy.

Pisherl, meanwhile, went about troubled. In the course of the days during which the Messiah-Ox gained weight, Pisherl lost it. He was continually disappearing from sight; continually wandering about in the woods, eating without appetite, and sleeping restlessly.

When we returned home to the forest at night, Anyella was waiting for us. She had taken to being quite friendly with us and taught us Christian Eden songs. In return, we taught her Jewish songs. Life was good around that pretty little angel. Pisherl could not tear his eyes from her. When it was his good fortune to sit near her, he turned crimson.

Once, on a Sunday, she invited us to go into the woods with her to gather strawberries. Her father, Ivan the forest ranger, was asleep. Anyella, as always, was very lovely, and it was impossible to refuse her. We went into the forest with her. Unable to fly because of the dense branches, we went on foot. Anyella laughed and sang and played tricks. From time to time, she bent to gather strawberries and dropped them into the pitcher she had brought with her. Occasionally, she broke off an entire cluster and held it to our mouths. Pisherl pulled the berries from the cluster with his lips. They flamed redder than the berries.

He went on with downcast eyes, silent, uttering not a word. I pulled him aside and asked if he wanted to be left alone with Anyella. His eyes lighted up. "You're a real friend, Shmuel-Aba. I'll never forget what you're doing for me. Sneak away so she won't know when you've disappeared."

I did as he asked. While Pisherl and Anyella were bent to the ground, engrossed in gathering strawberries, I disappeared. They did not come back until evening. Anyella was tired. My friend Pisherl was happy.

That night, when I woke from my sleep, I saw my friend standing at the window, holding something in his hand. "Pisherl, why aren't you asleep?"

"I can't sleep, Shmuel-Aba."

I jumped out of bed and went up to him. "What have you got in your hand?"

"Nothing. It's a secret, Shmuel-Aba." He closed his hand more firmly. I was annoyed and said, "Well . . . my best friend has a secret and won't tell me what it is. What's happened to our friendship?"

Pisherl, sensing my anger, came up to me and kissed me. "Shmuel-Aba, if I told you the secret, it would no longer be so beautiful."

"Never mind, Pisherl. I won't tell you any more secrets, either." I could see Pisherl struggling with himself, unable to make up his mind whether to tell or not. I stood by and waited. Pisherl opened his hand and I saw a lock of golden hair. "Did she give you that, Pisherl?"

"She did." I could tell that revealing his secret was very painful to him and I regretted what I had done. I promised myself that I would demand no more secrets from him. But now a devil had mixed into our friendship.

I crawled back in bed. I lay for a while with my eyes wide open. My heart ached curiously. From that night on,

Anyella plucked sprigs of strawberries
and held them to our mouths

whenever I saw my friend with Anyella, I disappeared, acting as if I hadn't seen them. I wandered around alone in the woods, or flew idly over the river. The days sped by; who can catch them?

Meanwhile, the Messiah-Ox put on more weight, though in truth not as much as before. There would still be plenty to do in the Jewish Eden before he would be entirely restored.

Pisherl left the care of the Messiah-Ox entirely to me, though it would be wrong to say that he sat with nothing to do. He went about in the forest carving the name "Anyella" on every tree. He wrote "Anyella" with a stick in the sand at the river's edge; and he whispered the name "Anyella" in his sleep. It may be that he wrote poetry too, but I didn't ask him and he didn't show me any.

Every Saturday, Saint Nicholas came with his sack on his shoulders. He rarely found Pisherl at home, so he had to confine his preaching and his presents to me. "Wouldn't it be better for you, Shmuel-Aba, if you were to stay here and be converted, eh? Our Eden is nicer than yours. You'll be as happy as can be here."

I would not be persuaded but replied, argument by argument: In the first place, how could I be so sure that his Eden was so nice? Had I seen it, after all? They hadn't let me stir in it so much as from here to there. "And in the second place, Reb Nicholas, aren't you forgetting the essential Jew? No small matter, that—the essential Jew!"

The old fellow smiled. "You're stubborn, Shmuel-Aba. And stubbornness is unpleasant." He went away unsuccessful. He came again, and again left with nothing.

To tell the truth, I was really worried by Pisherl. Now that he was gripped by his infatuation, Saint Nicholas might succeed in converting him. I prayed God that the ensuing weeks would pass swiftly, and that we would be home soon. Indeed, the weeks flew by, and the day neared when the Messiah-Ox was to be freed.

Later, my friend told me that he had continually prayed for the weeks to lengthen, but my prayer was preferred by God and the weeks had flown. "So you have good proof, Pisherl," I said, "that the Blessed One did not want you to become a convert and marry Anyella."

On the day that the Messiah-Ox was freed, Pisherl was a very sad angel. He was pale, and Anyella went about with tearstained eyes.

Saint Nicholas came very early in the morning with the news that the Messiah-Ox was ready to be turned over to us. We dressed and went outside. Anyella stood at her window, her eyes melancholy and huge.

"Good-by, Anyella."

"Fly well, Pisherl."

Two cuckoos called to each other in the wood, and the grasses sparkled tears. In Pisherl's eyes, drops of dew glistened. On our way, Saint Nicholas tapped with his stick; the wind lifted the edges of his garment. The sack on his shoulders rolled back and forth. Pisherl was nearby, continually casting glances behind him. Finally, one could no longer see the forest ranger's hut; it was hidden by the trees. Softly, I stroked Pisherl's wing and said, "Pisherl, forget her."

We came to the prison stable. The guard stood before it, his sword in his hand. A few paces farther on stood that monster, the angel Dmitri, holding a paper. We went into the stable with the guard. Dmitri removed the chains from the Messiah-Ox and threw them aside. Saint Nicholas took the sheet of paper from him and read aloud.

In the presence of Saint Nicholas, of Gregor Stasiuk, the guard, and of the gendarme angel Dmitri, we, the angels

Pisherl and Shmuel-Aba, take possession of the Messiah-Ox in order to return him again to the Jewish Eden.

We undertake to leave the Christian Eden quickly. We will not look about or dawdle anywhere on the way to the border. We understand that the gendarme angel Dmitri will accompany us the entire way, and that we are under his orders.

We signed this paper and made our preparations to go.

The Messiah-Ox could hardly keep on his feet, he had gotten so unused to walking. But that monster, the angel Dmitri, would not wait. He was a torment to our souls. "Giddyup, kikes!"

We drove the Messiah-Ox from his stall. Pisherl led him by one horn, and I by the other. Behind us flew the angel Dmitri. He twisted his mustaches and issued commands. "To the right, Jew-boys. Jew-boys, to the left."

It was a hot day. The Eden road was dusty (because of the Messiah-Ox, we went on foot) and our throats were dry. But the brute tormented us; he would not let us rest for a moment, would not let us drink so much as a drop of water. If the first journey with that anti-Semite was unbearable, the return trip was a veritable death. "And you were ready to stay with such monsters," I said to my friend.

The angel Dmitri imitated us, "Bread, bread . . . mommy, daddy . . . a black year." He kept cutting at the Messiah-Ox with his rubber truncheon.

We walked all that day. When night fell, we were still leading the Messiah-Ox by the horns. Barefoot and hungry, we went on, cursing our days and our years. The boundary was nowhere in sight.

"If only the monster shows up one day in the Jewish Eden, I'll teach him a trick or two," I thought. "Meanwhile, one must put up with it. And be damned before we'll let him know how much he's hurting us."

The angel Dmitri gave a sharp, vicious laugh, "Never mind, kikes. Never mind."

But these torments were as nothing. Toward midnight, Dmitri called out, "Halt." We came to a stop, trembling. With a twist of his mustaches, he commanded us to dance the *Mah Yofiss* dance.*

At first, we refused, but when he began to wave his rubber truncheon over our heads, we had no choice but to dance.

To this very day, when I remember that moonlit night, in the middle of the road, I'm overcome with revulsion. We danced, we turned, we flung ourselves about, and flapped our wings. We sweated pitcherfuls while he, the brute, flew over us, waving his rubber truncheon, wheezing with laughter.

When the dance was finished, and we could hardly stand on our feet, the monster took a piece of pork and ordered us to eat it. We resisted with all our strength, trying to make him understand that Jewish angels were forbidden to eat pork. But it was like talking to a wall; the monster insisted, and we had to taste it.

Grimacing, overcome by revulsion, we ate. Our grimaces seemed to please him. He shook with laughter.

We took up our journey once more, ashamed, degraded. I said to my friend, "Pisherl. Remember, no one in Eden must know that we ate pork. They'd wipe us from the face of the earth. Remember—not a word."

We walked on for the entire night and all of the next day. We did not arrive at the border until evening. We were so tired we could hardly stand.

The angel Dmitri signed over a paper to Saint Peter and took his leave of us. "Good-by, kikes."

* A degrading dance related to Polish mistreatment of Jews. The words are Hebrew for "How beautiful art thou . . ." and are taken from one of the songs sung at home on the Sabbath.

Old Peter put his spectacles on and began to read the document. While he read, we rested and caught our breaths. The Messiah-Ox stood stock still.

"A real Haman, that angel Dmitri," cried the rabbinical judge. "And such a fellow is allowed in Eden. God spare us from the like."

"Blessed is the name of God," breathed the rabbi. "So long as the Messiah-Ox was back at last in our Eden. I can just imagine the joy of the Zaddikim when he was brought back."

"You can't begin to imagine what went on. There was an entire parade. But I'll talk about that tomorrow, God willing. Now, I'm tired."

My father sat as if stupefied. He could not take his eyes off me. My mother ran up and kissed me, cursing the angel Dmitri meanwhile with powerful curses. "He should have dropped dead, that monster Dmitri. What agony he caused you! May he be flung from one end of Eden to the other until *I* cry, 'Stop.' "

She took me in her arms and put me in the cradle. I could just barely hear the rich man, Reb Mikhel Hurvitz, saying *sonderbar* several times.

I could still feel my mother's kiss on my cheek, and, as in a dream, I heard the visitors saying their good-by's to my father. I fell asleep.

XIII

The Parade in Honor of the Messiah-Ox

THE NEXT EVENING, when the rabbi, the rabbinical judge, and the rich man, Reb Mikhel Hurvitz, were gathered in our house, I made no lengthy preamble, but went on with my story.

As soon as we—that is, my friend Pisherl and I—were across the border into the Jewish Eden with the Messiah-Ox, we heard the sound of a trumpet. It was Gimpl, the border angel, letting everyone know that we had arrived, that the Messiah-Ox was now in Jewish territory once more.

Some dozen herdsmen appeared, as if they had sprung from the ground. They led a dozen fat, dignified cows on a rope—the wives of the Messiah-Ox. The cows were decked out in brightly colored ribbons in honor of the beloved guest, their husband, who had returned from abroad.

Gimpl, the border guard, signed to us to move aside. The first moment of meeting belonged to the family. The cows waved their tails, signaling their husband, greeting him in their language. "The darling is back. Sweetheart, we wept through the nights, not knowing what we might believe. Thank God that we see you well."

We moved off to one side and hid among the trees. Pisherl used the time to tell the herdsmen of our adventures in the Christian Eden. When we came out from behind the trees, we saw the Messiah-Ox licking one of his wives. It was Krassa, a pleasing cow with a black spot on her forehead.

"That's enough for today," said Gimpl, the border guard. "Now it's time to light the signal fire on the hill, to let the Zaddikim of Eden know the good news."

Several of the herdsmen went off. They climbed a high Eden hill that was close to the border. There they started a fire that could be seen for miles around. When the herdsmen returned, they told us that just as soon as they had lighted their fire, another fire appeared on a second hill, and one by one, other fires began to appear on all the hills of Eden.

"No doubt the Zaddikim already know that we're here, Pisherl."

"I couldn't care less," grumbled my friend. He could hardly keep on his feet.

I glanced back at the other side of the border and shuddered. There, on that side, was the monster Dmitri. But then I recalled that we had crossed over, and my spirits grew lighter.

I looked at the moon on the other side of the border, and then at our own moon, and I came to the conclusion that their moon was an abomination and ours was a moon to be blessed.

Gimpl, the border angel, whistled. We, together with the other herdsmen, gathered around him. "Time to bless the moon," Gimpl said, "and then it's bedtime. The parade in honor of the Messiah-Ox starts early tomorrow morning."

We blessed the moon, danced before her, and waved our wings. The moon beamed her pleasure, became fuller, brighter. The moon in the Christian Eden watched all this and almost burst with envy. In her fury, she hid behind a cloud.

Gimpl, the border angel, bade the herdsmen put the cows in one stall and the Messiah-Ox in another. "You understand, fellows. The Messiah-Ox is weakened. To put him in with the cows would be to tempt him. His health needs to be guarded. After all, an animal is an animal."

The cowherds did as the border guard told them. Then they lighted a fire in the open field and sat around it, singing:

> To fall asleep in a field,
> To bury oneself in the hay
> Is a thousand, thousand times better
> Than a bed where the fleas bite away.
>
> In the field, one hears the birds—
> Who knows how much to praise
> The cricket's song, and the wind
> Tickling in your nose.
>
> Ah choo, ah choo, God bless you;
> Ah choo, who can want more
> Than to watch the gentlewoman moon
> Coquetting here and there?

My friend Pisherl and I lay on the grass not far from the fire. We were counting the stars.

"How many have you counted, Pisherl?"

"One million and ninety-six."

"I make it one million and ninety-seven."

"You're lying, Shmuel-Aba."

"I'll take an oath, if you like."

"Swear."

*"Shikslekh, bikslekh."**

Pisherl grew sad. My oath had reminded him of the forest ranger's daughter Anyella. I poked him. "D'you know what, Pisherl? Let's start counting all over again."

"I don't want to, Shmuel-Aba."

I moved closer to him and touched his left wing tenderly. "Pisherl, believe me. Forget her."

Pisherl turned his back to me. I understood. I was wasting my words. He had to endure his grief. Then he would become a different angel.

Around the fire, the cowherds told each other stories. I tried to listen, but I could hear nothing. They spoke too softly—almost in a whisper. "If I can't hear, I can't," I said to myself and turned over with my back to the fire and fell asleep.

We were wakened in the morning by a terrible racket. We rubbed our eyes and looked about in a daze, not knowing what was happening. We went up to the cowherds who were talking in a cluster together. From them, we learned the following.

The minute the news had spread that the Messiah-Ox was back in the Jewish Eden, the patriarch Isaac hurriedly commanded horse and wagon to be hitched. Then he started for the border, desiring to check, with his own hands, whether the flesh of the Messiah-Ox that he had marked out as his was still fat.

The wagoner angel Zavl had lashed his horses unmercifully, halloing, and making his whip whistle. They had arrived at the border at the first crack of dawn.

* *Shikslekh, bikslekh*—A children's oath meaning, literally, "little Christian girls and little guns" (or, "toy guns").

"Open the stable," the patriarch Isaac said to Gimpl, the border guard. "I want to see the Messiah-Ox."

Gimpl refused. "The Messiah-Ox is tired. Let him sleep a while longer—an hour or two. Let him rest his weary bones."

The patriarch Isaac insisted. "Now, and quickly." He wanted to touch . . . with his own hands . . . because only that would convince him he was not dreaming.

We, that is, Pisherl and I, ran to the Eden stable. There we found the patriarch Isaac and the border angel. They were still quarreling. His shouts had already made the patriarch Isaac hoarse. "Open the door of the stable at once, this minute. Do as you're told." Finally, the patriarch prevailed. Gimpl opened the stable and let Isaac and his wagoner in. We peeked through a crack to see what they would do.

"Is there a chalk mark on the Messiah-Ox?" Isaac asked.

"Yes, holy rabbi," Zavl replied in his bass voice.

"Where is the mark, Zavl?"

Zavl, the wagoner angel, took Isaac's hand and led it to the spot where the chalk mark was. Isaac felt around and around, then shook his head. "That's not it. The place I marked was fat."

Zavl assured him that this was the only spot where there was a chalk mark. He saw no other marks. But the Messiah-Ox was not entirely himself. He was nothing but skin and bones. The patriarch Isaac sat down on the ground and wept. His tears ran down from behind his dark glasses.

Zavl the wagoner consoled him. "Don't worry, holy Zaddik. We'll put him out to pasture—this . . . how is he called . . . this Messiah-Ass."

I poked my friend. "Do you hear, Pisherl? 'Messiah-Ass.' What a donkey's head that angel Zavl has."

We watched as the patriarch Isaac stood up. The angel

Zavl brushed off his gabardine. "You'll see, holy Zaddik. In a week's time, he'll be his old self."

"From your mouth to God's ear," sighed the patriarch Isaac.

They left the stable. Zavl the wagoner led the blind Isaac by the arm. "Gently, holy Zaddik. There's a stone here."

The sun was already warm. Over our heads, birds were twittering. Blue Eden swallows were circling toward the sun. There was the scent of hay; of home. And I was happy to be alive. We said our morning prayers in the middle of the field and could hardly restrain our laughter at the mistakes that the angel Zavl made.

Soon after the morning prayers, the Eden musicians arrived. They had been sent to the border so that they might accompany the Messiah-Ox with music on the entire way back. Leading the musicians was the prophetess Miriam. She was small, lean, and freckled. It was a wonder to behold how she managed to carry the huge drum.

We, Pisherl and I, led the Messiah-Ox from his stall. His horns were decorated with blue and white ribbons. We waited for the signal to start.

Gimpl the border guard arranged the sequence of the procession: first, the musicians; after them, the Messiah-Ox with myself on his right side and Pisherl on his left. Behind us came the cowherds with the cows, and, finally, the patriarch Isaac in his silver coach.

Gimpl the border guard sounded his horn three times. The prophetess Miriam signaled to the musicians. The music exploded and we started off.

I am unable to express the joy that welled up in us. If you can imagine Purim and Simkhas-Torah in one day, then you'll have an inkling of one tenth of the holiday feeling we had.

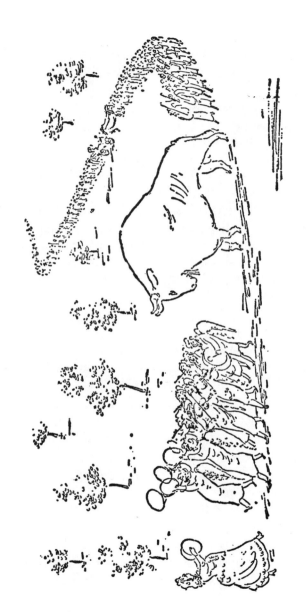

The music exploded, and we started off

The musicians went first, playing their instruments. Opposite us, the prophetess Miriam beat her drum and sang.

> Joy to your Zaddikim, Israel.
> Things were grim there, for a while.
> Now, all is well again,
> The Messiah-Ox is back again.
> We dance for joy, we weep for our good fortune
> And now, all's well again.

Anyone who has not seen the prophetess Miriam dance has not seen beauty in the world. She skipped the entire way, never resting for a single moment. She sweated pitcherfuls. Her wig slipped over to one side, but she, nothing daunted, beat on her drum and danced and sang without interruption.

> Blow the horns and sound the trumpets.
> The Messiah-Ox is here again;
> The Messiah-Ox has come again;
> How well for you, Zaddikim, how well;
> How well for you, how well.

The Messiah-Ox moved soberly and with great dignity, pacing step by step. He sensed that today he was in the spotlight, that the dancing and music were in his honor. He turned his head continually to his wives, who walked behind him. He seemed to be saying to them, "Do you see how they honor me?"

The cows nodded their heads in reply. "We always knew that you weren't a nobody." And in sheer joy, they dropped fragrant cowflops behind them.

Slowly, we approached the gate of the capital of Eden. "What's that shimmering over there, Pisherl? Do you see it?"

Pisherl peered intently. "I see, Shmuel-Aba. It's a rainbow that's been hung over the gate of the city. No doubt it's in honor of the Messiah-Ox."

"It's going to be some parade, Pisherl."

We halted before the city gate. The watchman angel, Simkha the Red, blew his horn: "Turoo, turoo, draw near; the Messiah-Ox is here."

The gates opened. The musicians withdrew to one side. Abraham the patriarch, the oldest of the patriarchs, came out. Behind him thronged the Zaddikim. In one hand Abraham carried a bunch of hay, in the other a cake of salt. He went up to the Messiah-Ox and handed him both. The Messiah-Ox sniffed the hay and gave the salt a lick. Then Abraham began a speech:

> In the name of the entire Jewish Eden, and in the name of the whole capital city of Eden, I greet you, Messiah-Ox.

Even a blind man could tell that Abraham had stage fright, but he controlled himself with all his might and went on:

> Though your running off has caused us considerable trouble, we will not punish you. You have been well punished by *them* already. But *we* receive you with joy.
>
> We have lighted rainbows on your account throughout the capital of Eden. Each rainbow costs a fortune, but who cares about money? We want to show you how dear you are to us. But see that from today and henceforth you play no more such dirty tricks. Behave, live out your time in happiness at home. After all, don't you forget it, it's greatly to your credit, you're the Ox of the Messiah, not a horse put out to hire. . . .

Out of sheer stage fright, the patriarch Abraham had begun to speak in rhyme. He turned white as chalk. His beard trembled as if it would blow away, but he held fast to it with his hand. Breathing heavily he ended: "Messiah-Ox, you're welcome among the blessed Zaddikim."

The Messiah-Ox waved his tail several times, expressing his thanks for the great honor being shown him. The cows behind him dissolved in sheer joy.

In back of the patriarch Abraham, pushing and shouting began. "Regarding what you've just said, I have a parable. Once there was a king who had three . . ."

"Enough of your parables, Preacher of Dubno," Abraham said. "Keep them for another time. This is no time for parables."

"You'll be sorry, Reb Abraham. It's a precious parable, and the moral is a golden moral."

"Not now. We don't need it," was heard on all sides.

The angel Simkha the Red blew his horn three times more, "Turoo, turoo. Draw near. The Messiah-Ox is here. Welcome."

The prophetess Miriam raised her hand. The musicians sounded their instruments and everyone, with the Messiah-Ox in their midst, marched through the gate into the capital of Eden.

Many-colored rainbows glittered everywhere. In the richer districts, each house had lighted one. In the poorer neighborhoods, there was one on every street. The lights glittered, shimmered. It made one dizzy to watch. The music played on. It was all very dreamlike.

In the Three Patriarchs' Allée, we stopped. This was where the real parade was to begin. An honor guard of the choicest Zaddikim formed around the Messiah-Ox.

"Attention!"

First to start off were the Eden roosters. Leading them was Solomon's cocky rooster. His commands could be heard. They were sharp, energetic: "Cock-a-doodle-do; cock-a-doodle-do."

Then, the Eden goats marched by. Their commander was a buck with huge horns and a beard that was strangely reminiscent of the one worn by Shlomo-Zalman the patch-tailor, Pisherl's father.

Then there was a company of oxen; and then, a company of ganders. Each of the creatures represented was the finest and the best of its kind. The parade lasted a full three hours by the clock. All that while, proud eagles wheeled overhead.

I, myself, heard Abraham the patriarch say to Isaac that in all the time he had been in Eden, he had never seen a parade such as this one.

"No one hitherto has been deemed as worthy as the Messiah-Ox."

A Zaddik who had been listening to the conversation called out, "When the Messiah comes, there'll be an even bigger parade."

"If only that time were come," sighed the patriarch Isaac.

After the huge parade, Pisherl and I went on, leading the Messiah-Ox by the horns. The honor guard walked at his side and behind us walked the entire throng.

The Zaddikim shoved and pushed. Each of them wanted to be close to the Messiah-Ox. They poked with their elbows and trod on each other's corns.

"Where are your eyes, uncle?"

"And yours, where are they?"

"Yipe. Ouch. He's stepped on my very best corn."

"You ought to leave the best one at home, Reb Zaddik."

"Who asked for your advice?"

I was intoxicated by the lights that glittered on all sides. "Pisherl. It's beautiful, eh?"

"Beautiful, you say. Fool. It's more beautiful than beautiful."

We neared the central square. The Zaddikim made a circle, linked arms and danced. The Messiah-Ox stared, his

"Once there was a king and he had three . . ."

eyes bulging. In all his life, he had never seen so many flying feet and beards.

"Faster, Jews. More joyfully, Zaddikim."

Those who stood outside the circle and did not dance clapped their hands. The prophetess Miriam beat her drum. The patriarch Isaac thrust himself into the center of the ring. One shoe off and the other shoe on, he leaped about, his beard flying every which way. He snapped his fingers and cried, "More happiness, more joy, Zaddikim." The patriarch Isaac felt that he had a stake in the festival. No one in Eden was such a connoisseur of beef as he. No one in Eden longed so intensely as he for his share of the Messiah-Ox.

The dance became faster, wilder. The Zaddikim could hardly catch their breath, but no one left the circle.

About twelve o'clock at night, the Great Banquet began. Tables were set out in the streets. Female angels in white aprons distributed roasted geese, chickens, and ducks. For the patriarchs, there was a small cask of Messiah wine. The Zaddikim drank to each other's health. They wished each other "life" and "only banquets in Eden." And they wished that their most recent sorrow might be their last; that nothing like the escape of the Messiah-Ox should happen again until the end of time.

Lovely female angels flew over the heads of the Zaddikim. Their flapping wings cooled the perspiring Zaddikim, who ate and drank and enjoyed themselves.

"Let's sing a little song," said the patriarch Abraham, brushing the crumbs from his beard.

"What do you need a song for," called the Preacher of Dubno, who sat at the other end of the table. "Much better if I tell you a parable. Once there was a king who had three—"

"Not necessary. Quit bothering us with your parable," the patriarch Abraham said, cutting him short.

The patriarch Isaac, who was on his third goose, put his knife down for a while and began to sing,

> What shall we eat at the Feast of the Messiah?

And the Zaddikim, in chorus replied,

> At the Feast of the Messiah
> We'll eat his Ox and the Leviathan.

From a great distance could be heard the drunken voice of the Holy Jew.

> Abraham, our forefather,
> Isaac, our forefather,
> Jacob, our forefather.

Pisherl and I also had a drop or two. We were a bit tipsy and held onto each other. "Pisherl, take a look at the moon. It's shaking. D'you see?"

"She's d . . . dr . . . dr . . . unk," Pisherl stammered.

"Do you know what, Pisherl? Let's fly around and sober up a bit." We rose up. Pisherl flew in zigzags, but he was still in control. Everywhere on the streets and boulevards, the Zaddikim sat at tables, singing songs, clapping their hands, enjoying themselves beyond measure.

Pisherl sobered up a bit. He tugged at my wing. "Let's fly to the Three Patriarchs' Allée. It's quieter there." We flew in the direction of the Three Patriarchs' Allée. Suddenly Pisherl stopped. "Do you see there, at the lamp post?"

I looked. Near the lamp post, there was an angel with a red beard. He was wobbly on his feet, and he was addressing the lamp post. "But it's Shimon-Ber. He's dead drunk, Pisherl."

"What else? Do you suppose Shimon-Ber could let an opportunity like this pass without tilting a cup?"

We descended lower and listened to what Shimon-Ber, who was standing before the lamp post beating his breast, was saying. "Good health and long life to you and to me. I'll divorce her today. Right away . . . that slob. And after the divorce, I'll marry you."

"He must really have swilled a lot. Now he wants to marry the lamp post," I said.

"Congratulations, Shimon-Ber," Pisherl cried, and we flew away.

The Three Patriarchs' Allée was also filled with drunken Zaddikim. They shouted, sang, and clapped their hands. The rabbi of Chortkov even danced in his underwear. "They are everywhere, and wherever they are, they're drunk," complained my friend Pisherl. "There's no place to catch one's breath."

We turned down another street—each time, the same thing. A third, a tenth . . . it was forever the same.

In Yohanan-the-Cobbler Street, it was quiet. We breathed more easily. We alighted there and went on, on foot. Though the air was not the best in the world, nevertheless we were able to breathe.

"Pisherl, just look over there." On the corner of Yohanan-the-Cobbler Street, there stood Maier-Parakh, our Talmud teacher. He had his cat-o'-nine-tails in his hand and he was teaching a pair of goats.

"Recite, scoundrels, or I'll whip you to death." The beards of the frightened goats trembled. The Gemora teacher, hardly able to keep on his feet, waved the cat-o'-nine-tails.

"He's drunk, Pisherl. I can't stand it, it's too funny." For a while, we watched our teacher as he taught the goats. I said to my friend, "Let's go wake his wife. When she sees her 'treasure' teaching the goats, he'll get his comeuppance."

Pisherl waved his hand. "I don't want to, Shmuel-Aba. I want to fly home. I'm tired. Come on with me."

We left the Gemora teacher teaching the goats and flew off in the direction of the Eden meadow where Pisherl's house lay. Just as we approached the Eden meadow, we noticed the Preacher of Dubno. He was walking thoughtfully. In the meadow, the Messiah-Ox stood grazing. The Preacher of Dubno walked up to him, patted him, and said, "I'll tell the parable to you. It's a precious parable, with a golden moral. Once there was a king and he had three . . ."

XIV

~~~~~

At the House of the Angel Zaidl, the Eden Photographer

AFTER THE GREAT PARADE and the great feast in Eden, there came the great hangover. The Zaddikim had gone a bit beyond their measure. For several days they went about with wet towels wound around their heads.

But one of them, the angel Shimon-Ber, was entirely recovered the next day, as if nothing had happened. He had even forgotten the promise he had made to marry the lamp post.

But who can be compared with Shimon-Ber?

In Eden, a series of dull days passed. The first day was like the second, the second like the tenth. The Zaddikim prayed three times a day. Their wives were beautifully decked out; the poor angels toiled; the rich ones ran things to suit themselves. The Messiah-Ox grazed in the meadow.

Dull, dull days in Eden.

Every Thursday was market day. Country angels from the surrounding villages brought in the best of everything. Eggs, butter, fruits, and vegetables; but particularly geese, ducks, chickens, and calves. Market day was Eden's most colorful day. But after the remarkable experience we had had, even market day seemed pale. All of Eden appeared to us as a single yawn.

If I was restless, Pisherl was more so. We loitered about the Eden streets and boulevards as if we were strangers. At least Pisherl had something to long for: the daughter of the forest ranger in the Christian Eden. But I—what had I?

We went back to Hebrew school to Maier-Parakh, the Gemora teacher. The cat-o'-nine-tails whistled over our heads. Silently, we prayed God to let the Messiah-Ox escape again so we might have something to do.

But the Messiah-Ox did not escape. He grazed quietly in the Eden meadow and gained weight. The pains he had endured in the Christian Eden had taught him a lesson once and for all.

And the days were dull, as dull as the Messiah-Ox's cud-chewing. Pisherl went about as in a dream. The boredom of the days in Eden sharpened his longing and made it more painful. He did not reply when spoken to; if he was shouted at, he started up as from a trance, "Ha! What?" Truly a distracted angel.

One day, Maier-Parakh, the Germora teacher, interrupted him during a lesson. "Pisherl. What are we reading?"

Pisherl started up as if he had been wakened. "We're reading. . . rabbi. . . we're. . . reading . . ."

The Gemora teacher was furious. His eyes narrowed. He gave the cat-o'-nine-tails a shake. "We're reading," he mimicked, "we're reading . . . Let's just see what you've got there in your hand, you scamp."

Pisherl would not open his hand. The Gemora teacher caught it up and forced it open. He broke into a grin. "So, that's how it is, wise guy. A lock of a girl's hair. Hmm. Hmm. Now, whose could it be? Let's just give it a thought. Your mother has black hair, and so does your sister. Hmm. Hmm. But this is blond hair . . . so . . . *so!* You're playing with a Christian girl's hair. And that's why you don't know what we're reading."

Pisherl turned red. The rabbi regarded the lock of hair. Then he sniffed it. Suddenly, he said, "Pisherl, bend over."

Pisherl shouted and shrieked and cried, but to no avail. The rabbi beat him steadily, saying meanwhile, "*So* you *will* play with a Christian girl's *hair,* you scoundrel. Twelve, thirteen, fourteen, fifteen. *So* you *will* play with forbidden things. Fifteen, sixteen, seventeen . . ."

The teacher sat down again at his place. He rolled the lock of hair into a twist of newspaper, making a cigarette of it, which he then lighted and began to smoke. "A rare cigarette . . . mmmm . . . mmmm. It's been a long time since I've smoked such a fragrant cigarette."

Pisherl watched, stunned, while the memento Anyella had given him turned to smoke. The smoke curled up and out through the window, turning to nothing. He gritted his teeth and swore revenge in his inmost heart. He would repay him for this. Maier-Parakh the Gemora teacher would have cause to remember him for all the days of his life.

For several days after this, Pisherl did not come back to Hebrew school. I was very uneasy about him. "Perhaps he's sick," I thought, and went to his home where I inquired. "Where is Pisherl?"

"What do you mean, where? In Hebrew school," said Hannah-Deborah, Pisherl's mother. I understood at once that Pisherl had told no one what had happened. He had let his mother think he was still going to Hebrew school, but he was wandering about the streets and boulevards—alone.

He returned to school on the sixth day. His face was

glowing. He took me to one side and whispered in my ear, "Do you know what, Shmuel-Aba? Abinadab the postal angel brought me a letter today."

"From whom, Pisherl?"

"Dope. Don't you understand? From her. From Anyella."

"From the Christian Eden?"

"I was lucky, Shmuel-Aba. No one was home when the postal angel brought the letter. Otherwise, I'd have been questioned: 'What's this? A letter from the Christian Eden, all of a sudden?' "

"Show me the letter, Pisherl."

"You can't read it, Shmuel-Aba, but I can let you have the stamp."

Pisherl removed the stamp from the envelope and gave it to me. It was green, with a picture of a dove with a little cross on its neck.

"Be careful, Shmuel-Aba. Don't let the Gemora teacher catch you with the stamp. You'll be beaten."

"Nuts to him, Pisherl. But you be careful. Hide the letter well. The Gemora teacher is just likely to roll himself another cigarette."

"He'll find it, like hell, Shmuel-Aba."

That day Pisherl was a whiz at his lessons. He was a completely different angel, unrecognizable. The Gemora teacher, Maier-Parakh, thought his whippings had helped make the difference. The fool couldn't know that a few written words from a blond "forbidden thing" could accomplish more than a million whippings.

In the evening, when we left the Hebrew school, Pisherl could contain himself no longer. He showed me his letter. It was only a few words, "Pisherl, when are you coming back again?—Anyella."

"Do you know what, Shmuel-Aba? We have to see to it that the Messiah-Ox escapes again."

"He won't want to escape, Pisherl. Think! There, in the Christian Eden, his feet were bound, and he had half a pound of hay per day. And here, what a parade! Do you think that the Messiah-Ox can't tell the difference between good and bad?"

"So what's to be done, Shmuel-Aba?"

"Let's wait a bit more. God knows what may yet happen."

That evening we flew all over Eden, happy as we could be. We caught butterflies and played with them. The butterflies trembled in our hands. We let them go, laughing with all our hearts.

We flew over the house of Zaidl, the Eden photographer. On a bench before the house sat Zaidl's three daughters, Shifreh, Sloveh, and Traineh—a trio of high-bosomed old maids with sour faces. They were talking to each other, and, as was their habit, they were gossiping about everyone in Eden.

On the roof of Zaidl's house, some dozen or so black tomcats with upraised tails and green eyes prowled. In Eden, the cats were known as "the angel Zaidl's grandchildren" because Zaidl's daughters raised them.

The angels and the Zaddikim who lived in Zaidl's neighborhood went about irritable and sleepless because the tomcats yowled so at night and would let no one get any sleep. On the other hand, if mice appeared in anyone's house in the neighborhood, it was to the angel Zaidl that the owner came. "Reb Zaidl, be good enough to lend me a cat."

Zaidl shrugged his shoulders. "D'you think they're mine? Ask my daughters."

"Reb Zaidl, the rats have gnawed my holiday wings. Be

good enough to lend me a cat, if even for a single night. You'll be buying grace for yourself." The angel Zaidl shrugged his shoulders as if to say, "Why are they harassing me? Are they *my* cats? If they were mine, I'd have drowned them in the Eden river long ago."

The neighbors said, "That Zaidl—a villainous angel." But they were mistaken because the real villains were his daughters, the three old maids who raised the tomcats and then, out of sheer spite, would do nothing to help their neighbors in a moment of need.

The angel Zaidl, the Eden photographer, led a miserable life with his daughters. Whatever he said they paid as much attention to as if he were a howling dog. If any one of them turned stubborn over anything, he immediately gave in, and was satisfied—indeed, considered himself lucky that they did not tear one of his Purim plays into a thousand bits and pieces.

Ever since his wife, the angel Simeh, ran off with a Christian angel to the Christian Eden, leaving him with the three girls, Zaidl had found some consolation in the writing of Purim plays. He was as careful of them as of the eyes in his head, and, as we know, whoever might come to his shop heard a play, whether he liked it or not.

"Pisherl, let's visit the angel Zaidl."

"I don't want to, Shmuel-Aba. He'll bore us with one of his Purim plays."

"But we promised him, Pisherl."

"So he'll call us liars."

Zaidl's daughters noticed us flying about over their heads. They called up, "Why are you flying around over the roof? You'll scare our cats."

"Good. It will keep them from the evil eye."

"Pisherl, cut it out. To fall into the clutches of those

daughters is worse than falling into Hell." I called down to them, "Is the angel Zaidl at home?"

"He's home," they shouted. "Come down, scoundrels. Can't you see that our cats are scared?"

I tugged at my friend's wing. "Come on, Pisherl."

We descended. Zaidl's daughters stared at us and we at them. Close up, we could see how really ugly they were. "Where is your father?" we inquired.

The three ugly angels burst into laughter and poked their elbows into each other's ribs. They were disgusting. We went into the photography studio. The angel Zaidl was sitting at a table retouching a negative. The lamp over the table burned weakly and Zaidl's shadow, complete with long hair and the glasses on his nose, danced about on the wall like a character in one of his own Purim plays.

"Good evening, Zaidl."

The angel Zaidl was delighted to see us. He set two stools before us and asked us to sit down.

"A lucky thing you've come, lads. Only yesterday, I finished a new Purim play, 'Noah in the Ark.' You'll like it, boys. Maybe you'd like a little something. That is, what can I serve you? A glass of tea and preserves? Shifreh . . . Sloveh . . . Traineh. Where are you? Put on the samovar. We have guests."

Outside, the three beauties paid no attention to their father. They did not even deign to reply, but continued to sit, as they gossiped about Eden. The angel Zaidl had to go to the trouble himself of lighting up the samovar. He came back into the house, his hands and face smudged, and groaned, "Well—they won't stir a finger about the house, those daughters of mine. They obey me in absolutely nothing. That's how they obey the commandment 'Honor thy father. . . .' No use talking about it. If they had only run off with their mother, I wouldn't need to put up with such shameful behavior."

"What's that you're grumbling about, Pop?" one of the daughters shouted through the window. "Something wrong again?"

"Who's grumbling, Sloveh? You're imagining things, darling. What . . . grumbling . . . may my enemies perish . . ." said the angel Zaidl apologetically.

Outside, the daughters laughed aloud. The cats on the roof yowled and the angel Zaidl poured glasses of tea. "Drink, fellows, and then I'll read you my play about Noah."

We sipped the hot tea. Zaidl sat down opposite us. Pisherl asked him, "Why don't you marry your daughters off?"

"You ask me why?" sighed the angel Zaidl. "It's easy to ask and hard to get them married off. Who do you suppose would want them? They're not good-looking and nowadays the very least of the angels expects a fortune as a dowry. Where would I get it—eh? Nowadays aren't the good old days. In those days you used to marry off daughters without noticing it. Today—give 'em money."

"He's a real *shlimmazel*," I thought. "His wife, though he wanted her, runs away, and his daughters, whom he'd be glad to be rid of, stay behind. When I grow up," I decided, "I'll write a Purim play about him."

Zaidl was growing uncomfortable. The tea-drinking was taking too long. He could hardly wait for us to finish up.

"Well now, will you have a little more tea?" he inquired, and, frightened lest we should say yes, he added, "Too much tea in the summer is unhealthy."

We pleased him by saying we didn't want any more. He invited us into the living room, where it would be better for reading. Here, in the studio, the table lamp hurt one's eyes.

We went into the living room. For a while, Zaidl busied himself at a drawer and then he took out a manuscript. We sat down on one of the three beds that stood in the room. Zaidl sat facing us on another bed. He coughed once and said, "Don't interrupt me in mid-reading, fellows. You'll see. You'll enjoy it."

"We're ready to listen, Reb Zaidl."

The angel Zaidl buried his nose in the manuscript and began to read. On the roof, the cats yowled.

NOAH IN THE ARK

The Zaddik Noah is lying on the ground, dead drunk. Ham and Japheth come in.

HAM:	Japheth.
JAPHETH:	Eh?
HAM:	D'you see our father dozing there?
JAPHETH:	Soused with wine As much as he could pour, Now he's snorting like a bear.
HAM:	D'you know what? Listen here, Let's tease him just a little.
JAPHETH:	And with a straw him tickle So he'll think the fleas are biting.
HAM:	No, no, no, no; God forbid, It will drive our father mad, And we'll get a "nine-tails" whipping.
JAPHETH:	If not that—what then?
HAM:	Oh, I've got a plan.
JAPHETH:	Let's hear it.
HAM:	I think we should uncover him.
JAPHETH:	Agreed. But hush, let care be taken. We don't want our Pa to waken.

They approach on tiptoe. They uncover Noah who sleeps like one dead. Then they take each other's hands and turn about him, singing:

HAM AND JAPHETH: Baa, Papa, baa.
                    We see your "you know what,"
                    Completely, all of it;
                    Come young and old, come running, see
                    Noah's "you know what"—a joy.
                    Come and dance about.

At that moment, Shem comes in. He's carrying a Bible under his arm. Seeing his dear brothers, he grows angry.

SHEM: Beat it, rascals. Scram, I tell you.

HAM: You crooked nose, you go to hell, you.

JAPHETH: Jew-boy impudence, unheard of . . .

SHEM: And I'll tell our daddy on you.

HAM: Good, that's all you need, Goddamn
                    you.

The Zaddik Noah wakes up at this point. He rubs his eyes, looks about in all directions and spits three times.

NOAH: Ugh. I dreamed that I was sitting
                    On the house-of-study roof
                    Two or three or four long days
                    Studying God's book.
                    Suddenly, a crash and bang . . .

He clutches his heart and turns to his sons who stand around him.

NOAH: A glass of water, I feel sick.

Shem runs off and returns bringing a glass of water.

SHEM: Take it, Papa. Drink.

Noah drinks the water. He feels a bit better. He pinches Shem's cheek.

NOAH: You're a good fellow, Shem.

Noah takes the cat-o'-nine-tails down from the wall. His sons seat themselves around the table. Melodically, Noah inter-rogates them on their lesson.

NOAH:	What chapter's being read this week?
JAPHETH:	"Go thou and leave . . ."
HAM:	No. "Blow thou and sheave."
SHEM:	Papa, I know . . . I know. "And these are the generations of Noah . . ."
NOAH:	Then all of you recite aloud.

The Zaddik Noah waves the cat-o'-nine-tails. The three boys bob up and down over their Bibles, chanting:

THE THREE SONS:	These are the generations of Noah: Smoke goes up the chimney, Vigor comes from brandy.

Enter, a delegation of dogs. They wag their tails and bark.

DOGS:	Bow, Reb Noah, wow. We are God's creatures, oh. We'd like for you to feed us Because your stingy missus, Your old and stingy missus, Has forgotten all about us.

The dogs move to one side. A delegation of pigs comes in. Each pig holds out its right forehoof.

PIGS:	Hail, Reb Noah, hail. Hear us for a while. Indeed, we're flesh you mustn't touch But your stingy missus, Your old and stingy missus, Is a true-born witch.

The pigs move to one side. Two white cats come in. They are very skinny. They meow:

CATS:	Meow, Reb Noah, meow. Please inform your *Frau* That milk in a small dish

> For Mitzi, my betrothed one,
> And a pot of sour cream
> I wish, I wish, I wish.

The angel Zaidl could read no more. The cats on the roof had begun such a yowling that he could not hear himself speak. We stopped up our ears. The angel Zaidl was simply beside himself. The "Noah play" trembled in his hand and he groaned. "It's bad enough to be tormented by my daughters—at least they're daughters. But to be tormented by cats! That's beyond human endurance."

The three daughters came into the room. The cats ran leaping before and behind them. One cat climbed into my lap. I shoved it away. Shifreh, the oldest daughter, threw me a dirty look and muttered, "May it be your head you push, little angel."

The second daughter began to drive us from the room. "Go on, boys. It's already late. It's bedtime."

The angel Zaidl was unhappy. No sooner had he found an audience for one of his Purim plays than his daughters, a curse on them, came in and wouldn't let him finish.

"Well, what are you waiting for, rascals." The oldest daughter blew out the lamp with a wave of her wings. We were left in the dark, with no alternative but to go. We felt our way along the wall and found the door only after great difficulty.

"Good night, Reb Zaidl."

The angel Zaidl groaned deeply. He still sat with the Purim play in his hand. His daughters scolded, threw the bedclothes about. In the dark, the green eyes of the cats glittered.

Once outside, we smoothed out our wings and breathed deeply. The heavens were filled with stars. Above our heads a little cloud cruised. "Do you know what, Shmuel-Aba? Let's float around a bit on that cloud," said Pisherl.

We flapped our wings and flew up. The little cloud was floating slowly, unhurriedly. Where in the world would it hurry to, and why?

We grasped the edge of the cloud and in a trice were aboard and riding. Pisherl was delighted. His eyes glistened. Seen from below, no doubt, they too looked like stars. He sang,

> To ride on a cloud
> Over earth is so sweet;
> It's a million times better
> Than horses so fleet.
>
> The best horses grow weary,
> The fleetest grow weak;
> We can ride on a cloud
> For a day and a week.

I looked down. The houses of the Eden capital looked like toys. I tried to find the houses and villas of the Zaddikim. Pisherl continued to sing.

> Giddyup, cloud horse, giddyup.
> Fly on; fly on, don't you stop.
> Fly on, and don't let us drop;
> Giddyup, cloud horse, giddyup.

"It's too bad, Pisherl, that the angel Zaidl isn't with us. Here on the cloud, he'd be able to finish reading his Purim play and forget the yowling of those cats."

"Who needs him—that *shlimmazel*," said Pisherl with a wave of his hand. "Let him sleep where he is, in good health."

"Still. You might have some pity on him," I said. "And the Purim play was nice enough."

Pisherl continued his singing:

> Giddyup, cloud horse, giddyup.
> Giddyup, horse in the cloud,

> Let's fly where the white moon spider
> Is spinning her silvery thread.

We floated about on that cloud for some time. Near midnight, we jumped down. It was high time, too. The cloud was drifting in the direction of the Turkish paradise. We waved to the receding cloud and sang:

> Cloud, greet Hagar there,
> And Ishmael her son.
> And tell them both to send us
> Tobacco in a tin.

We flew back home and settled down beside the Eden meadow. I said good-by to my friend. "Remember Hebrew school tomorrow."

Pisherl laughed,

> Where Maier-Parakh, at the least,
> Is as pious as a priest.

He went into the house and I flew off toward home. Flying over the angel Zaidl's house, I paused. There was nothing to be heard. The angel Zaidl, the three ugly daughters, and the dozen cats slept. The Purim play lay in a drawer, ashamed.

I pitied the poor *shlimmazel*. But there was nothing I could do to help except to sigh for him.

A star fell over Zaidl's house. "Just his luck," I thought. "And maybe, his bad luck." I went on home, to sleep.

XV

Magicians in Eden

MAGICIANS APPEARED in Eden and no one knew where they came from. On a fine evening, they entered our city riding on a peasant cart. There were two men and a woman. The men both wore red Turkish fezzes and the woman wore a blue dress with red polka dots.

The cart stopped and from it the Turks dragged boards and began to work. In an hour or so, they had built a stage in the middle of the square.

The woman went about the streets beating a drum and inviting everyone to come and see the magicians whose like was not to be found in any of the three Edens. Mohammed the Prophet had bestowed an order on them—a gilt crescent on a yellow ribbon. Anyone who was skeptical could come to the square the following morning when he could see for himself.

The woman spoke in a bass voice. The Zaddikim could have sworn she was a man disguised as a woman. "A man's voice," said the rabbi of Lublin, "and the clothes of a woman. So? What is she?"

"You said it yourself, 'What is *she?*'" said the rabbi of

Apt, "and *she,* in ordinary usage, denotes the female. Conclusion, we are dealing with a woman."

"We! Who's *we?*" the rabbi of Lublin said angrily. "Maybe *you're* dealing with a female, in which case don't use the locution *we,* rabbi of Apt."

"Right! Right!" chimed in the other Zaddikim, who had been listening to the quarrel. "The rabbi of Lublin is right. Where does he get off saying *we* out of the blue?"

The rabbi of Apt was apologetic, "It's just a manner of speaking, gentlemen. I meant no harm, God forbid. What's all the anger for?"

The holy Jew offered a compromise. "According to all indications, gentlemen, this is an androgyne. Since the voice is that of a man and the clothes, to be sure, are those of a woman, and since the two together, gentlemen, do not go together, as you will agree, there remains the conclusion: an androgyne."

The woman with the man's voice acted as if she heard nothing and went on with slow steps, beating her drum. "Come and see. Come and see. You've never seen the like in your lives. Come see the great magicians. Tomorrow at ten o'clock, see Mohammed Ali and Ali Mohammed. If you don't see them tomorrow, you'll regret it. Their like is not to be seen everyday—not even in Eden."

We—that is, Pisherl and I—were sitting together at the house of Maier-Parakh, the Gemora teacher, doing our lessons. All at once, the Gemora teacher set the cat-o'-nine-tails aside and said, "Magicians."

That was all his students needed to hear. They scattered —some flew out the door, some out the window, leaving Maier-Parakh alone in the room, gaping.

We flew after the woman with the drum, wondering at her masculine voice and her blue dress with its red polka dots. I nudged my friend, "It's going to be merry in Eden."

Pisherl was delighted. He had heard a great deal about magicians, but he had never seen any. Tomorrow, he would see them with his own eyes. How lucky he was.

The Turks and their woman caroused all night in the tavern At the Sign of the Zaddik Noah. Even Shimon-Ber had to confess that the magicians had hollow legs, that they really knew how to drink. You ought to know that the angel Shimon-Ber is very loathe to praise any one on this account; but when he says of someone, "He knows how to drink," then you may be sure that it's as real as gold. Shimon-Ber is an expert in these matters. The angel Shimon-Ber became very friendly with the Turkish magicians. The night he spent drinking with them At the Sign of the Zaddik Noah was, according to him, one of the best in Eden.

"So there I am, flying past the Eden tavern," Shimon-Ber related, "and I hear singing. 'Who can it be?' thinks I to myself; and I decide to have a look-see. When I open the door, first thing I see is the Turks, the magicians. There are two bottles of whiskey on the table; several empties are rolling about on the floor. The Turks, their arms around each other's shoulders, are singing.

> Wine is good,
> But whiskey is better.
> Two barrels, well-filled,
> Grant us, O Allah.
>
> Great art Thou, Allah,
> Of all things, the greatest;
> There are drinks in the world,
> But whiskey's the greatest.
>
> Then let us drink up
> Till we make the night say,

"Allah be praised
And hip, hip, hooray."

"As soon as the Turks saw me," Shimon-Ber went on with his narrative, "they became silent, thinking I was a police angel or something. I waved my wings and pointed at the bottles. 'Drink. Drink up, magicians. Drink in good health.' The Turks were delighted at my words. They invited me to join them at the table and to drink with them.

"Well, you know how it is," said Shimon-Ber, scratching his neck. "It's not nice to refuse an invitation. So we drank to each other's health till dawn. They really know how, those Turks. But that woman—a curse on her—drank better than the men. She poured the stuff down with no effect."

Everyone felt that Shimon-Ber was not telling the whole truth. No doubt he had drunk with the Turks. The angel Shimon-Ber was not likely to refuse that kind of invitation. But the fact that later Shimon-Ber flew about all over Eden stopping everyone to tell them, for heaven's sake, to go and see the magicians—that seemed extremely strange.

The older female angels whispered, "The woman bewitched him. Those Turkish beauties are great witches."

"Dumb females," the angels said scornfully. "How quick they are to discover witchcraft. As if Shimon-Ber wouldn't sell all of Eden for a glass of whiskey."

An old angel with gray wings said, "Who doesn't remember how Shimon-Ber pawned his wings at the tavern and went about on foot for a year until we gathered alms for him so he could redeem them again?"

Whatever the explanation, the fact remains that Shimon-Ber flew all over Eden, praising the magicians to the skies, urging the angels, large and small, to go see them.

"Where are we going to get money for tickets?" the little angels asked.

"Get yourself a little straw and push the coins out of the alms boxes," advised Shimon-Ber. "Or you can steal the money out of your father's cashbox at night."

All of Eden was in a turmoil. No matter where you were, no one talked of anything but the magicians. I couldn't sleep a wink the entire night.

Just as soon as day broke, I dressed, said my morning prayers and was off to my friend Pisherl. In the wink of an eye, Pisherl dressed himself. We went out of the house on tiptoe. Pisherl showed me several coins he had swiped from the Maier-Bal-Ness alms box. "That should be enough for two tickets. One for you and one for me, Shmuel-Aba."

In Eden, everyone was still asleep. We flew over the deserted streets and boulevards. There was not a dog to be seen, much less angels or Zaddikim. Even the angel Shmaya, the policeman, whose duty it was to patrol the Elijah-the-Prophet Boulevard, was lying in some kitchen with a wench, leaving the entire boulevard unguarded.

Flying past the patriarch Abraham's villa on the Three Patriarchs' Allée, we saw him in his prayer shawl and *tefiln*. He was just finishing the *Shmone-Esre* prayers.

At one of the open windows of the patriarch Jacob's villa, Billah was emptying the chamberpots. At another, Mother Rachel drew the curtains aside and yawned full into the face of the morning.

"Pisherl?"

"What, Shmuel-Aba?"

"Let's take a little stroll down to the Eden river."

We flew to the Eden river. There we skipped so many stones into the water that at last the Leviathan awoke. We saw his head break the surface of the water and we ran away, singing,

> Leviathan, Leviathan,
> If you mean to be a groom
> Get a top hat made of silk.
> Then, the children will be quick,
> One and all, to sing together,
> "Where's the groom? The groom's in water.
> What's the groom? The groom is wetter."

Luckily for us, the Leviathan could not chase us. If he had, he'd have swallowed us down without a blessing, and we would have seen the light of day again only at the coming of the Messiah. To be left lying in the Leviathan's belly for so long a time was not a bright prospect.

We flew back to town. The streets were filled with Zaddikim and their wives and children, all of them hurrying. Everyone wanted to be at the square as early as possible to get a good place from which to watch the magicians. The patriarch Jacob was out with his entire family, his four wives and twelve sons. His daughter Dinah was, as always, powdered and painted like a doll.

The air was filled with angels, large and small, all of them with coins in their hands. Only a few of the inhabitants of the poverty-stricken Bal-Shem Alley and some of the workers of the Yohanan-the-Cobbler Street stayed at home.

We—that is, my friend Pisherl and I—also began to hurry. We flew at top speed, not infrequently bumping into a grown angel or a young female angel. We had just time enough to excuse ourselves; to say "pardon," and then we were off again.

We had something of an incident with the angel Tcharneh the Prattler. Pisherl accidentally bumped her, and the witch, as was her custom, instantly began a series of wild complaints, cursing at the top of her voice, as if we had destroyed her best cloak. "May your eyes fall out, you bastards. They crash into one and think if they say 'pardon' that's all there is to it. May you fly to Hell, together with your 'pardon'; and come back when I send for you." Tcharneh the Prattler went on and on. Once she gets started, she knows neither end nor measure. Fortunately, the angels flying behind us hurried her on in her turn.

"Don't block the way, Tcharneh. Fly on, or let us fly on. The magicians will start on time."

The square was filled with Zaddikim. The female magician in the blue dress with the red polka dots was collecting money in a plate. Shimon-Ber flew about making change for the Zaddikim. "Faster. Hurry up. They're going to start," he urged.

We arrived just on time. The Turk Mohammed Ali was standing on the stage pulling ribbons from his nose and his ears. He put the ribbons into a large box, and then—one, two, *"Allons, passez!"* The box disappeared. The Zaddikim stared, their mouths wide open. They shook their heads and clicked with their tongues. "Oh my. Oh my. A real wonder."

But all of this was nothing compared with what the second magician now did. Even if you forget about the way he swallowed fire the way the Zaddikim might swallow stuffed cabbage, this Ali Mohammed performed miracles. The Zaddikim had never seen the like in their entire lives; and, be it said, the Zaddikim were connoisseurs of tricks.

Ali Mohammed took the fez from his head, bowed before the company, and smiled. He asked anyone in the gracious audience to throw something into the fez. They hesitated for a moment, unwilling to risk anything, but when King Solomon removed the gold sealing ring from his finger and threw it into the fez, Queen Esther followed, throwing in the little gold mirror that Ahasuerus had given her at their wedding; the patriarch Abraham dropped in his precious snuff box; Mother Sarah added a gold earring; and the patriarch Isaac threw in his cuff links.

Ali Mohammed shook the things up well in his fez. Everyone stared, waiting to see what would happen. Those who had dropped things into the fez trembled with anxiety. Ali Mohammed smiled his usual smile, then *"Allons, passez!* One and two, shmay and dray!"* He turned the fez upside-down. It was empty. Queen Esther all but burst into tears. "My little mirror. My little golden mirror. King Ahasuerus gave it to me at my wedding." Ali Mohammed smiled and, bowing before the patriarch Abraham, he said, "Begging your pardon, Reb Abraham, would you give your beard a shake?"

The patriarch Abraham shook his beard and, wonder of wonders, Esther's golden little mirror fell from it.

"And you, Reb Solomon," Ali Mohammed said to Solomon, "Mother Rachel is standing three rows behind you. Will you be good enough to glance at her finger?" Indeed, King Solomon's ring was found on her finger. Mother Rachel was embarrassed because, in everyone's presence, a stranger's ring was removed from her finger.

The patriarch Abraham's snuff box was found in the bosom of Zilpa, the patriarch Jacob's servant-wife; the patriarch Isaac's cuff links were found in the prostitute Rahab's left stocking.

Everyone was astonished. They laughed and praised the great magician Ali Mohammed who, judged by his skill, could have been one of the greatest Zaddikim in the province of Galicia.

Suddenly Mother Sarah wrung her hands and cried, "My golden earring! Woe is me, my golden earring is lost."

Ali Mohammed pointed his finger at the Preacher of

Dubno, who was standing in a middle row. "Shame on you, Preacher of Dubno. Since when have you taken to wearing women's earrings. Be kind enough to give the earring back to Mother Sarah." The gold earring hung on the Preacher of Dubno's left ear. It was removed with great difficulty.

The Preacher of Dubno was thoroughly excited. "Gentlemen, I have a parable that is just to the purpose here. Once there was a king who had three . . ."

"No need for parables, Preacher of Dubno. We've come to see tricks, not to hear parables," shouted the audience.

"You'll be sorry, gentlemen. The parable is a rare parable, and it has a rare moral," urged the Preacher of Dubno. But he made about as much of an impression on them as last year's snow. The eyes of the audience were turned to the stage where there now stood the woman with the mannish voice. Now it was her turn to show what she could do.

The woman with the mannish voice said, "Raneh, kapaneh, alleraneh." She was suddenly enfolded in seven colorful veils. The veils were enough to dazzle the eye. The Zaddikim stood with their mouths open.

The woman commanded the seven trembling veils, "You, white veil, fly to Mother Sarah. You, red veil, to Mother Rebecca; you, gray veil, to Mother Rachel, and you, blue veil, to Mother Leah."

The four veils separated themselves from the rest and fluttered over the heads of the audience until each of them had found one of the women. "Now, come back," commanded the woman with the mannish voice; and at once, the veils left the women and flew back to her.

The woman with the mannish voice said, "Raneh, kapaneh, alleraneh," and the veils disappeared. No one knew what had become of them.

The two Turks returned to the stage. They took their

places opposite the woman with the mannish voice. Speaking in German, one of them said to the other, "This woman belongs to me. A proof? her hair is golden." And all at once, the audience saw that the woman's hair was, indeed, golden.

But the second one argued, saying, *"Allons, passez.* The woman is mine. The proof? she has red hair. Am I telling the truth?" We looked at the woman with the mannish voice. It was true. Now, she had flaming red hair.

The magicians continued to quarrel. One said one thing, the other another. And each time, the woman's appearance changed to suit the argument. Back and forth they went until one cried out, *"Allons, passez.* Fairy, be gone!" And the woman disappeared. The two fellows made obscene gestures at each other; then, bowing before the audience, they said,

> Now the show is done,
> Clap hands, everyone.

The Zaddikim did clap hands, but none of them wanted to leave. They expected more tricks, but the magicians evidently thought they had done enough. They took their stage apart and packed up their things. The woman with the mannish voice appeared again, as if she had sprung up out of the ground. Their things were placed in the wagon. The woman beat on her drum and the wagon started off. The magicians were on their way once more. Where, nobody knew.

On the wagon, the Turks waved their red fezzes, bidding the audience adieu. The older one cried, "Farewell, Zaddikim. We'll come again, with brand new tricks." The entire audience accompanied them to the city gates. The patriarch Abraham said good-by in the name of the entire

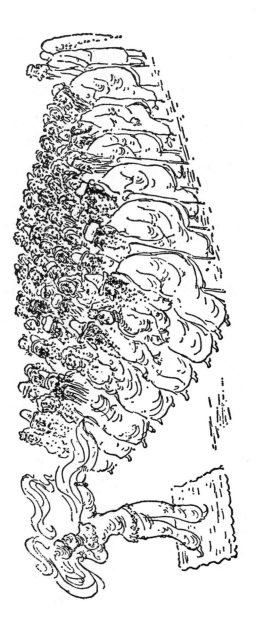

The woman with the mannish voice performed tricks with veils

city and invited them to come again to drive boredom out of Eden. "You'll earn real grace thereby," he said.

The woman with the mannish voice was so touched by his words that she embraced him and would have kissed him.

"Uhg. Pfooh. Aagh." When the patriarch Abraham would not let her kiss him, she had no alternative but to climb back into the wagon.

One of the Turks called to the horse, "Giddyup." And the wagon started off. The Zaddikim looked after it, waving their kerchiefs for as long as it was visible; but when the wagon merged into clouds and highway, they looked at each other. "Gone. Really and truly gone."

"A pity. A pity," they all sighed, and started home each one to his own household.

My friend Pisherl and I also flew homeward. I missed the merry magicians intensely. In my imagination, I watched again the enchanting performance of the three Turks. My heart ached.

"When do you suppose the Turks will come again, Pisherl?"

"How should I know? What am I, anyway? A prophet, Shmuel-Aba?"

"Do you miss the Turks, Pisherl?"

"Like the side of a barn," Pisherl muttered; but I could tell he didn't mean it. He was just putting up a front. In truth, he missed them as much as I, and perhaps even more.

Flying over the holy Three Patriarchs' Allée, we heard cries of distress. We settled to earth to find out what was happening. We could hardly believe our ears. The holy patriarchs were running around like poisoned mice. Their beards were disheveled; the holy mothers were wringing their hands, weeping and wailing. "We've been robbed.

The houses are completely emptied. Not so much as a thread left."

Mother Sarah was harassing Father Abraham, accusing him in the most violent language. "He had to have Turks. Meanwhile, thieves took everything in the house. *Your* Turks. As if anything decent could come from your Ishmael."

Abraham begged her, almost with tears in his eyes, "That's enough, Sarah. You'll see, the thieves will be found. Just stop it."

In the other streets of Eden, similar scenes were taking place. The Zaddikim, and their wives, ran about angrily. Their weeping and wailing reached into the seventh heaven.

"That thieves should sneak into Eden," wailed the rabbi of Apt.

"It was the devil who brought those Turks. I wish they had broken every bone in their bodies before ever they got here," cursed Sarah-bass-Tuvim, her cap flying around her head like a crazed dove.

A little Zaddik with a yellow beard suggested, "Maybe it's all a Turkish trick."

"A Turkish trick, do you say? By all means, a trick. Those Turks have indeed tricked us—showing us magic and meanwhile stealing us blind."

"Sarah dear, enough," pleaded the patriarch Abraham. "What good does it do to take it all out on me. It won't help find the thieves."

The Eden police in their green uniforms came flying. The Zaddikim began to reckon what had been stolen.

"All the bedclothes; the silver candlesticks; the gold-handled brush; a wedding ring."

"The mirror on the wall, the Sabbath shawl. Even my Zaddik husband's slippers."

"The holiday clothes, a silk umbrella, and a sack of blessings."

"The silver hanging lamp. The kerchief I inherited; the prayer shawl from Leipzig, with the golden fringe."

"The silver case for my smelling salts; my oldest daughter's silk stockings, and my niece's bridal linen."

"The hammock out of the garden, a snuff box, a handkerchief, and, if you'll excuse the expression, the bedpans."

The Zaddikim added up, the wives helped out, and the Eden police wrote it all down. It was some theft! Not a single house had been spared.

The police inventory lasted all day. The Zaddikim were so distracted that they forgot to say their evening prayers.

"The Turks must be caught," said the patriarch Abraham to the chief of the Eden police.

The chief of police gave his mustaches a twirl, as if to say, "You may be a great Zaddik, Reb Abraham, but as regards thievery, I know better than you."

Someone mentioned Shimon-Ber's name. The chief of police pricked up his ears. "What about the angel Shimon-Ber?"

"Shimon-Ber spent an entire night carousing with the Turks. In the morning, he helped them collect money from the little angels who came to watch the magicians."

"Aha!" said the chief of police, giving one half of his mustache an upward pull. "Aha." He had practiced this "aha" a dozen times. Then he commanded the angel Shimon-Ber to be brought to him.

Two police angels went off. They found Shimon-Ber drunk in the tavern and brought him back with them. He could hardly stand on his feet.

The chief of police began to question him, telling him hoarsely that there was nothing for it but to confess quickly where the Turks were to be found. The angel Shimon-Ber swore that he knew nothing. The Turks had treated him to whiskey, and he had accepted. Perhaps the police angel could show him where in the laws of Eden it was written that when a Turk treats, it is forbidden to drink.

The chief of police shouted at him. He told him, curtly and harshly, that he would tolerate no dirty tricks. He was an expert in such things. Shimon-Ber was an accomplice to the theft. The proof? He had collected money from the little angels at the behest of the Turks.

Shimon-Ber became frantic. He shouted so loudly that many a Zaddik's soul sank to his stomach. One could say that he was a drunkard. Let them say it. But a thief. A thief! Anyone who said he was a thief . . . he'd, he'd . . . he'd show him. And he grabbed the chief of police and shook him so hard and so long that the chief could hardly catch his breath. "A thief, you say," shouted Shimon-Ber, "a desperado! I'll break your wings, you—you—you—"

He was released the next day. Shimon-Ber insisted that he had thought the Turks were Turks. How could he have known that they were thieves, scoundrels? He had had a drink or two—that was all; how was he to know that a theft would be the result?

Among the Zaddikim, there was despair. They slept on bare mattresses; ate with their fingers; and swallowed their tears. The police searched and investigated. Every day, they made a new report. The stationery store run by the angel Hannah ran out of paper, but still the thieves were not found.

"How will it end?" the Zaddikim asked the chief of police. "Is the loss irrecoverable, Excellency Adon?"

The chief of police twisted his mustaches and smiled cunningly. "What are you talking about—'irrecoverable.'

The Eden police don't know the meaning of the word *irrecoverable*."

A Zaddik declared, "Thievery ends at the gallows."

And once again, there was searching, investigating, inquiry. Fugitives were arrested and released; then others were arrested.

What finally happened, whether the thieves were ever caught, I can't say because a few days later, my friend Pisherl brought me the news that Shimon-Ber was to take me away from Eden so that I might be born on earth.

I was silent. Opposite me, the rabbi sat as if carved out of stone. The rabbinical judge sat with his eyes staring out of his head. The rich man, Reb Mikhel Hurvitz, sought for something to say about these remarkable stories of Eden. Finally, he said, *"Sonder . . . sonderbar."*

My father sat, his elbows on the table, his eyes wide with wonder.

"A strange world, that Eden," the rabbi said. "A world of contraries, of brutes, and thieves. Woe is me. How can it be possible, little boy? I just can't believe that all these things you've been telling us are true."

"Everything I've told you is true. I saw it with my own eyes."

"Maybe you've imagined it," said the rabbinical judge. "You thought it up, and now you think it's true. After all, who can believe that the Zaddikim are sleeping on bare mattresses; and that their wives are unable to bless the Sabbath lights because their candlesticks have been stolen?"

"Maybe it *is* imagined," the rabbi said, clutching like a drowning man at a straw.

"It is not imagined. It is the plain truth. Maybe the Eden you paint for yourselves is imaginary—something you thought up. The Eden from which I come is real, and though it has its faults, it is lovely, just the same. The proof of that is I miss it, and, if only it were permitted, I'd go back at once."

My mother ran up to me, caught me in her arms and pressed me to her heart. "What are you saying, my darling son? What do you mean, you're ready to go back to Eden? My little treasure, you'll stay with your mother. I'll scratch the eyes out of the first one who tries to take you from me."

"Well," I thought, "there you have it. No sooner do you start something with an earthly mother, then she's ready to scratch your eyes out. They think this world is such a bargain that it couldn't possibly pay to leave it. It's not for nothing that in Eden there's an expression, 'She is good, and foolish, like an earthly mother.' "

The rabbi stroked his snow-white beard and asked, "How does it happen that they sent you down to be born and not your friend Pisherl? You were just the same sort of little angel as he."

I said that apparently I was not a true angel, but rather, a temporary angel. The difference between the true and temporary angels is that the true angels cannot be born on earth. When a true angel sins, he is sent for a time to the World of Errors or to Hell. In Hell he must shovel glowing coals with his bare hands until his punishment is finished.

The rabbi stood up. His whole body trembled. He said to my father, "Faivl. Prepare for the circumcision, Faivl. I advise you to name him Shmuel-Aba, just as he was called in Eden."

My father agreed, "Of course. Shmuel-Aba. What else could it be but Shmuel-Aba?"

My mother would not put me down. The rich man and

the rabbinical judge took leave of my father. "You've been sent a jewel, Faivl. Guard him like the eyes in your head. A boy like your Shmuel-Aba is a real treasure."

My mother hugged and kissed me. Tears glistened in her lovely eyes. "My treasure . . . my gold . . . my Shmuel-Aba."

The guests kissed the *mezuzah*. The rabbi said aloud, "Good night. God willing, we'll meet again at the circumcision, Faivl."

My mother put me in my cradle. For a long while, my father wandered about the room.

His unbelieving shadow flickered on the wall.